I Still Dream of Horses

of Horses

A girl, her horse and the stories of their lives

Leanne Heffernan

*For Consuela, for my beautiful children,
and for all of the souls who were born inexplicably
in love with the magic of horses.*

Dear reader,

Before you begin, there is something I would like you to know about the stories contained within this book: they are all strongly based on actual events. The places, the animals and the people you will read about were all real, and all of the events within these stories actually happened and have been retold exactly as I remember them; what I hope makes these stories really come to life is that I have adapted them to be told to you through the eyes of my horse, Consuela. I have used her personality traits and mannerisms to describe our adventures to you straight from the horse's mouth, from her point of view, and as she tells our stories you may find yourself getting to know her quite well along the way.

For the privacy of those who played a part in our stories, I have changed everybody's name except for my own. The names of all the animals, however, remain the same.

I hope that you will enjoy reading about our adventures, dramas, tragedies and above all, our extraordinary friendship, as much as I have enjoyed writing about them all for you. This book is a tribute to everything Consuela was and everything she brought to my life, and it's a pleasure to have you along for the ride.

Leanne.

Chapter 1 – No ordinary day

It was 1998, and it was just another Sunday as far as I was concerned. I was woken at the crack of dawn by the sound of magpies carolling in the early morning light, and I could feel the first gentle rays of the sun slowly creeping over me creating a pleasant warmth across my back. It had been a hard winter, and it was such a relief to feel the days getting longer, and to taste the sweetness in the green spring grass. I remember walking slowly across the paddock, dragging my feet and feeling quite relaxed and ready for the new day. When I reached the dam I dropped my head to drink and as I gulped down the cold water, I suddenly sensed that something would be different about today.

The sun had been up for a few hours and I was all very busy dozing under my favourite tree when I heard the sound of a car door slamming. I looked up to see who had interrupted my nap, and was pleased to see it was Veronica. Immediately the thought of a bucket full of tasty chaff and pellets entered my mind, and my stomach growled at me all the way to the paddock gate. As she approached I saw that her hand was behind her back, and I knew that she was hiding my halter and lead from me. You see, in my younger and cheekier days I would run away if I knew that someone wanted to catch me. It would usually mean I was going to be ridden and let's face it, I was getting far too lazy for that sort of business. On this particular day I didn't try to run because my mind was still clouded with that vision of feed, or maybe even a biscuit of hay!

To make it clear that I would very much like to be fed, I offered Veronica a small whinny and stood quietly while she put my halter on. I was to find myself bitterly disappointed, however, because a moment later another car pulled up. A woman got out of it and began talking to Veronica, and as they looked at me and discussed how tall I was, how old I was, where I had been, what I had done, I got a sinking feeling deep in my heart. I knew exactly what was happening- I was being sold. Again.

As I stood there that day tied to the gate I was barely aware of my surroundings. I knew that Veronica was saddling me up, and I could feel the strange woman staring at me, looking me up and down and dissecting me with her eyes. But none of that really registered, because in my mind a hurricane of questions and sadness was brewing. What had I done wrong? Why were they sending me away? I had tried to be good, I didn't kick, I didn't bite, and I had forgotten the art of bucking and pig-rooting years ago. But try as I might I couldn't understand why yet another owner was saying goodbye to me. It's a difficult thing for a horse to endure and I had been in this position more times than I cared to remember.

For the rest of the day people came and went, and I have to say I hadn't liked any of them. I guess that when you're 18 years old with a swayback as bad as mine you can't expect to be selected for Her Majesty's stables now, can you? There had been noisy and downright unpleasant children who had pulled at my mane and yanked on the reins and screamed orders at their mother from my back. There had been a man who seemed to think he was a cowboy but clearly had no idea how to actually ride a horse, and there was a particularly unfriendly woman who did not even bother to greet me or pat me before she climbed onto my back as if she was scaling Mount Kosciuszko.

Needless to say, by mid-afternoon I was very tired and very fed up with my situation. I was just beginning to think that nobody else was coming and I might finally get that feed I had been dreaming of, when to my absolute dismay another car pulled up outside the gate. Sighing gently through my nostrils I watched as 3 people got out of the car and walked towards me. There were two adults, who stopped and stood talking to Veronica. The third was a young girl who only stopped long enough to politely say hello before she headed straight in my direction. I stood watching her approach, hoping that she wasn't another spoiled pony clubber wanting to whip me over jumps and yank on the reins until my mouth was red and sore.

The girl walked the last few steps to me slowly and held out her hand for me to sniff. She spoke to me in a friendly gentle voice and ran her hand down my neck, reassuring me and letting me know that she would be kind to me. Veronica came over and helped her adjust the stirrups and then the girl mounted and we wandered out into the paddock.

It was as if she sensed I was very tired and she didn't push me to work too hard for her. We walked across the grass, past the dam where I had my morning drink, and she softly asked me to trot. She didn't jab me harshly in the ribs like most of the others that day; she was much more of a gentle casual rider and I didn't mind trotting on for her. We did a slow lap of the paddock, and I mustered a little bit more energy on the way back to the gate and cantered with her. When we got back to where the adults were standing, she dismounted and stood beside me asking Veronica questions and talking to her parents. While they talked she held my head in her arms, stroking down my face and rubbing my cheeks. I was so exhausted that I fell asleep standing there with her that afternoon, as my fate was decided by the people surrounding me. The girl, Leanne, would be my new owner. She was 14, and getting her own horse had been her greatest wish for as long as she could remember.

I still recall how calm I felt with her, how we both knew we could trust each other from the second she had first touched me. It had been a long stressful day for me but by late afternoon I wasn't worried anymore. I slept all evening and dreamt of rolling green fields filled with rich juicy tussocks of grass, and buckets of lucerne chaff sweetened with the finest molasses. There was a change in the air that day.

Although I didn't know it yet, that Sunday was the beginning of an amazing friendship that would last for more than a decade. It was destined to be filled with many happy days spent in the sun, hard times and heartache, a little bit of hope and even a miracle or two.

My name is Consuela and I would like to tell you a story.

Chapter 2 – A new lease on life

The weekend after I first met Leanne, I was loaded onto a big yellow truck and taken to my new home at Macarthur Park paddocks in Canberra. It was government-managed public agistment and was very different to where I had been living before, on a property at a place just outside Canberra called Hall. I only had one horse in the paddock with me there, but when I got to Macarthur I found myself sharing with almost 30 other horses. I was terrified and for the first week I was kicked, bitten and chased by nearly every one of those unfriendly nags. Eventually I settled in and learned the pecking order, and it wasn't too long before I knew which horses to avoid.

Every day Leanne would come to visit me, and I was extremely impressed that she always brought a treat for me when she came to catch me. Sometimes it was a carrot, or some bread, maybe an apple, but every now and then she would bring my favourite– an over-ripe brown squishy old pear. Thank goodness Veronica had passed on this secret to her! The thing she didn't mention about my love of pears was that you need to take a few steps back while I am eating this delicious treat. In my excitement and bliss I had a tendency to dribble everywhere, lovely sweet pear juice dripping down my chin, and to clean myself up I liked to rub it all over the nearest person. She figured that out soon enough though, after a few sticky juicy face-rubs from me!

When I first went to live with Leanne, I'd had a difficult winter and was looking very poorly. I was skinny, you could see my ribs through my dirty dull winter coat, I needed my feet trimmed very badly, I needed to be wormed and I couldn't remember the last time that my teeth had been filed. When I had lived at Hall, Veronica could only come to see me once or twice a week so now with my daily visits I was feeling quite spoiled! Rain hail or shine, Leanne would arrive every day to feed me, brush me, pick out my feet, and tell me all about her day and how much she had looked forward to seeing me. I was nervous for the first couple of weeks and constantly ran away when I saw her coming with my halter. But after a while I realised that there was no need to run from this quiet, softly spoken girl. She was giving me the love and care I had been needing so badly and soon I was watching the sun move across the sky, waiting for the time of day when I knew she would be there.

As the weeks went by I started to shed my awful wormy winter coat and my darker sleek summer coat came through. I was putting on weight and starting to look very healthy indeed. Not only did I look better on the outside, but I was feeling better on the inside too. Leanne and I were forming a bond, a friendship, and I hoped that I could look after her as well as she was looking after me.

I remember the look on her face the first time that I whinnied at her. She was walking through the dry crunchy summer grass, holding my halter at her side, having no need to hide it from me anymore. As she got closer she called out to me, 'Suelaaaa, c'mon!'. At the sound of her voice I instantly raised my head, pricked my ears forward and gave her a friendly whinny. The reaction I got was like a child seeing fireworks for the first time. A huge grin of delight spread across her face and she cried out to me 'hello beautiful girl!'. I could sense her happiness and delight and as she put the halter on she patted me and talked to me as if she was having a conversation with her best friend. Then I realised that this young girl was doing exactly that, she was talking to her best buddy, smiling and laughing as if we'd known each other all our lives. In the short time we had been together I had become the world to her, and she was now the world to me too.

It is a unique relationship that forms between a girl and her horse. I don't think there is anything that can compare to it, and I felt that I must be the luckiest old mare in the whole world. At 18 years old, many horses would be coming to the end of their lives, or being turned out in a paddock to retire and fend for themselves. But I had just had a new door opened before me, a brand new lease on life and I was loving every minute of it.

Life in a pecking-order society such as a mob of horses can be tough and the first time that I received a nasty bite from one of the other horses in the paddock, Leanne panicked. She had brought me into the yards to feed me and as she started to brush my grey speckled coat, she spotted a wound on my rump where one of my cranky paddock mates had sunk their chompers in and left a big set of teeth-marks cut deep into my skin. Don't get me wrong, it had hurt, but it was nothing serious. When Leanne saw it she got so upset, fussing and worrying and even talking about whether I would need the vet! Thankfully one of the women there reassured her that it was nothing to worry about, so she sprayed some antiseptic on it and started to calm down. I have to admit I felt rather special knowing that somebody cared enough about me to get so distraught over a little bite.

On Christmas Day Leanne came to see me, as always, but on this special day she had come bearing gifts! Not only had she bought me a present, but she had wrapped it in colourful Christmas paper and written my name on the gift tag. When she caught me in the paddock she kissed me on the nose and wished me a merry Christmas, feeding me carrots as we walked to the yard together. She tied me up then stood beside me and excitedly unwrapped the gift, making sure that I could see it as she went.

Inside the bright paper was a lovely new halter to replace the old worn-out one that I had been wearing for so long before she met me. It was clean and shiny new and every section of it was a different colour. Red, blue, green, yellow, purple, and clipped to it was a brand new lead rope too. If I could talk, I would have been speechless.

She put it on me and I swelled with pride, feeling like a model in a horse gear catalogue. But then came the icing on the cake – literally! She had made me a special horsey Christmas pudding, and it smelled delicious. She presented it to me smiling from ear to ear but I sensed that she was worried I wouldn't like it. Not much chance of that, I had thought as I took a huge bite out of it. She had made it out of torn up pieces of bread, chopped apple and carrot, sugar and apple sauce. It was sticky and sweet and I had never had such a fantastic surprise in my life. I was disappointed when she only let me eat half of it, because she wanted to go for a ride. It seemed that she still had one more present for me, and it turned out to be a brand new Wintec 100 all-purpose saddle. It was much prettier and a lot lighter than the stock saddle she had been riding me in previously, but it was a saddle nonetheless and I wasn't all that thrilled really!

I was still thinking about eating the rest of my pudding when she started to saddle me up, and my daydream was rudely interrupted by a sharp pinch on my belly. Ouch! The new girth on that Wintec was pinching me! I pinned my ears back in protest and took a step back, swishing my tail so she would know I was very upset. Unfortunately, she didn't seem to realise what I was trying to tell her and she continued to tighten the girth. It pinched again, hot and sharp on my poor belly and it was then that my instincts took over. I didn't want to, I couldn't help it, but when it pinched me again, I snaked my head around and bit her hard on the arm. I felt terribly guilty but it was my nature and she had been hurting me!

She jumped back in surprise as she cried out and rubbed her arm, and as she scolded me I saw tears of pain welling in her eyes. I really didn't mean to upset her but it was a reaction and it was one of those natural behaviours that go along with being a horse!

Unfortunately for my dear inexperienced friend it took her the best part of a week to work out why I had suddenly become a nasty unfriendly horse. At first she had thought maybe the saddle didn't fit properly and it was hurting my back. She bought a thicker saddle cloth to try, and she started to tie me up on a very short lead while she was saddling me so that I couldn't reach around to bite her. I had given her some fantastic bruises because my teeth were sharp, I had a strong jaw and I knew how to use it! Before that new saddle came along I had been enjoying our rides together, following the equestrian trails through the hills or flying over jumps on the grass at Macarthur. Now I dreaded seeing Leanne carrying her gear towards me. Then one afternoon I was steeling my nerves for another pinching session- my ears were back, my nose was wrinkled up.... but when she tightened the girth it didn't hurt. I still had my cranky face on but I turned my head to see what was happening, feeling much less hostile. Thank goodness, there was a whole new girth around my belly, and it hadn't pinched me at all! It took another few weeks before I stopped pulling nervous unhappy faces at saddling time, but she never used that nasty pinchy girth again.

Summer was a complicated time of year for me. Being an appaloosa meant that I had extremely sensitive skin, and I suffered terribly from sunburn. My entire muzzle, the skin all around my eyes, on my withers, and under my tail was pink and all through the long hot summer months Leanne would have to smother me in zinc cream to protect me from getting horribly sunburnt. I hated having it rubbed around my nostrils; the smell bothered me so I would try my best to get away when I saw that tube of cream in her hand. But she was wise to my naughty behaviour and I never got away with it. It was for my own good anyway and when I got sunburned it hurt, so after a while I gave up and let her do it. Once she was done it seemed there was more zinc on her than on me, and I always managed to wipe even more off onto her before the day was through. She never yelled at me for it though, she seemed to like my cheeky sense of humour.

Another problem with the hot weather was the flies. There are always thousands of them wherever horses are and they buzzed around sticking to my eyes and itching my skin. The day Leanne bought me a fly mask it was like going to heaven; the mask kept the annoying insects away from my face and it was such a relief to me that I could have kissed her! It did get a little itchy once I had been wearing it all day though, and when she took it off in the evenings I would rub my face and eyes all over her. I was stronger than I realised and several times I nearly pushed her over. It felt lovely scratching my itchy eyes on her but it made quite a mess considering that my nose was painted white with zinc, and I was responsible for many of her shirts being ruined.

One of my fondest memories of summertime at Macarthur was when Leanne would take me swimming. There was a dam in a large empty paddock only a 10-

minute ride away and several of us would go there to cool off. Leanne and a few of the other girls would ride us down bareback, and we horses would stand in the dam and paw at the water with our front feet. It was tempting to get down and roll in the cool murky water but I never did, knowing that my dear friend was still on my back. By the time we had finished splashing around in the shallows and soaking each other, all the girls were laughing so much they could barely balance on our backs. But the best part was when Leanne took me all the way into the dam, where it was so deep that I would have to swim to the other side. I would push through the water with my power-ful legs propelling me across towards the shallows on the other side. As I swam, Leanne would float above me with her arms around my neck, letting me carry her safely back to the land. The only part of me that was visible was my ears, eyes and nose, and I would snort loudly as I swam to keep the water out of my nostrils. Once the girls had gotten tired of playing in the dam we would all wander home together, walk-ing happily on a loose rein, drip-drying in the warm evening breeze. I remember feeling very peaceful and content, knowing that when we got back to the yards I would be given a lovely big feed to eat while Leanne hosed the mud from my legs and rinsed the dirty dam water from my coat.

In these happy days before Leanne finished school

and went out into the world, we would spend hours together building our special friendship. She used to take my bridle to school with her, and at 3:00 she'd catch the bus to the paddocks so that she could ride me bareback every afternoon. Then she would give me my dinner and sit up on the wooden fence beside me while I ate. She often stayed until well after dark, when she would sit staring up at the stars and I would listen to her talk. She would tell me stories about her confusing teenage life and ask me if I knew the solutions to the problems troubling her. Of course she knew I would not answer her but she seemed to enjoy our conversations anyway. I could always tell if she was sad or upset and I did my best to cheer her up with a whinny or a good face-rub on her clean shirt.

These simple moments were not only strengthening our friendship; they were creating memories and fulfilling the dreams of a girl who had wished for a horse just like me all her life. Sometimes when I am drifting off to sleep I think about these special times and it makes me smile deep in my heart; I fall asleep knowing that I have a best friend who loves me more than life itself.

Chapter 3 – News, and it's all bad

Before Leanne's dream of owning a horse came true, she would go trail-riding at a riding school called Forest Park. Nearly every weekend she would go for a one-hour ride, either with a friend or by herself. She often told me that some riding-school horses were so quiet that they were like robots and may as well have just had an on/off switch to control them. At Forest Park they ran programs in the school holidays where you would go there all day every day for a week and do lessons, trail riding, jumping and general horse care exercises.

Leanne and a few of the girls at Macarthur took their own horses along with them one summer holidays instead of using a school horse. She kept telling me how much fun we were going to have, but I was dreading it! From the moment we arrived I was extremely unhappy. This unfamiliar place smelled of strange horses, manure and dust and there were noisy children everywhere, which made me very nervous. To make matters worse, I was forced to live in a stable for the week and I hated it. Leanne did her best to make me feel at home, bringing my rugs and my favourite brush with her and giving me lots of treats to eat, but I am as stubborn as a mule when I want to be... which makes sense I guess, considering that mules are half horse! Anyway, to show her that I wanted to go home and I meant business, I decided to go on a hunger strike. When she arrived in the morning after my first night there, I hadn't touched my water and I had barely eaten any of my food. My hay was deliberately strewn across the stable and mixed in with the sawdust as an act of defiance. I was very pleased to see that this made her rather annoyed, as the hay kept clogging up her rake while she tried to pick up the manure I had kindly deposited for her. She was very worried that I hadn't eaten or drunk anything all night, and I was hoping that she would decide we should go home. But I was to have no such luck, because she still saddled me up and off we went to the indoor arena for our lesson, with my empty hungry belly growling at me all the way.

For most of the week I behaved like a silly cantankerous old cow. It was fun to carry on like this when I was usually so well-behaved! Nothing that we had been doing was any great challenge to me anyway; I could have done it standing on my head. Mind you, that's almost what I did at times. I planted my feet and refused to move when she asked me, I wouldn't canter for her, I cat-leaped over the jumps with no timing at all, knocking the poles everywhere, and I shied for no

23

reason. I was having great fun making her cross and the whole time I was hoping she would give up and take me back to my paddock at Macarthur. On the third day she thought that some oats might put a bit of life back into me, so she fed me a few handfuls first thing in the morning when she arrived. They must have worked, because all I wanted to do for most of the day was pig-root. The week dragged by horribly for both of us and needless to say, my plan was a success and she never took me to one of those programs again!

One sunny afternoon not too long after we had returned from Forest Park, Leanne got a phone call that would make her heart leap into her throat. She was over at a friend's house when Carrie rang on her mobile, sounding very upset. Carrie was one of her friends who kept her pony at the paddocks with me. 'You better come to the horses quick' she said. 'Consuela is lying down in the paddock and she can't get up. She's sweating really badly too.' Straight away the word 'snakebite' popped into Leanne's head and by the time she got to Macarthur she was extremely stressed and upset. Carrie and her sister had managed to get me on my feet and they had slowly led me down to one of the holding yards while they were waiting for her.

I'm pleased to say it wasn't a snakebite; it was actually a very nasty injury caused by one of the other horses in my paddock, but I had no way of telling Leanne that. I could barely walk and I wouldn't put any weight on my near-side back leg so I had decided to lie down and rest. Leanne had tears in her eyes and she ran to me and crouched down at my side. She patted me for a second and then grabbed me by the halter and forced me to stand. The pain was excruciating, I was trembling and sweating and as I reluctantly got up I groaned loudly with pain and unhappiness. She noticed immediately that my hock was horribly swollen and within seconds she was dialling the vet's number on her mobile phone.

While she was waiting for the vet to arrive she led me, one slow step at a time, to the wash bay, where she turned on the hose and let the cold water run over my poor swollen leg. It helped to numb the pain just a little and I was grateful that she was there trying to help me. About 45 minutes later the vet drove through the gates and parked in front of the wash bay where I stood balancing on three legs. She asked Leanne questions as she examined my aching hock, and then she made me walk up and down so she could watch how I moved on the injured leg. I heard her telling Leanne that it looked like a very nasty sprain, and that she should give me painkillers and rest me completely for at least 2 weeks. After that she should try to start walking me for 20 minutes every day and slowly work up to some gentle trotting to build the strength back up in my leg. She gave Leanne some 'Bute', a drug which would help with the pain and bring down the swelling, and then she got into her 4-wheel drive and off she went to attend to some other sick and injured horses. At this point I had never wished I could talk so much in my life, because from the amount of pain I was in I thought it had to be more than just a sprain. The painkillers started to kick in then and I drifted off into a restless sleep.

For 2 weeks I rested, and my hock had barely started to improve. Leanne began taking me for slow relaxing walks, hoping it would help to heal my poor leg. At first it was awful, I was so lame that I almost had to hop and we never got very far before I was exhausted and starting to sweat. But as the days turned into weeks I started to feel better and after a while I didn't limp at all. About 8 weeks after my injury had happened Leanne started to ride me again, just walking though, and she was very careful not to overdo it and risk hurting me all over again. I was barely lame anymore but my hock still remained very swollen. Things seemed to be slowly looking up for me when I was hit with another nasty blow.

I had always had quite weepy watery eyes and one day while Leanne was giving them a wipe with a damp cloth she noticed a lump right on the inner edge of my eyelid. She had a closer look, trying to see it better while I was throwing my head around in protest and making it difficult for her. The lump didn't really hurt me, it was just very uncomfortable and I didn't like her touching it. She became very worried and rang the vet to tell them what she had found.

Because I'm a pink-skinned appaloosa and we are very prone to skin cancer, they sent my usual vet straight out to see me again. She seemed very concerned and decided it would be best to do a biopsy and find out if it was cancerous or not. To do this they had to sedate me, because they were going to be using a very sharp needle right next to my eyeball and they didn't want me to move unexpectedly and hurt myself. The vet gave me the sedative and within minutes I was woozy and sleepy. I vaguely remember them sticking the special needle in and removing a tiny sample of the lump, but in my drugged state it felt like I was floating in a thick foggy haze. When I woke up I had two tiny stitches in my eyelid and the sample they had taken was on its way to the lab for testing.

I think it was about a week later when Leanne got a call from the vet. They had very bad news; the lump was something called a squamous-cell carcinoma, which was a nasty type of cancer. It could spread very quickly through my bloodstream and they wanted me to have an operation to remove it. When Leanne told me this terrible news as she brushed me that evening we were both very scared. It had been enough of a shock to my system when I hurt my leg and now this was even worse.

A few days later everything was arranged and a truck arrived to take me to the equine hospital for my surgery. I was about 20 years old at this stage and it was quite risky to give an older animal a general anaesthetic, so Leanne was feeling extremely nervous. Once she made sure I was settled in and comfortable, Leanne went home to wait for the call to say my operation was over. I felt very afraid in that strange place; there were all sorts of odd smells and unfamiliar sounds. The horse in the stable next door to me told me that he had been there for a week because he was a racehorse and he had hurt his leg doing track work one morning. I was very impressed with him! He said he was worth a lot of money, plus I thought he was rather handsome too. I was glad to have him keeping me company and he told me not to worry because the vets there were very good and would be nice to me.

Shortly before my operation was to start, one of the vets came to examine me. Walking around behind me, he noticed that the hock I had injured previously was still extremely swollen. He was worried and rang Leanne to ask her about it. She told him what had happened and how the lady vet had come to see me, and he said he thought it was unusual that it was still so swollen. They decided to take some x-rays since I was already at the hospital, and when the films were developed they showed that I had in fact fractured my hock. It had been broken! To add insult to injury, they could also see on the x-rays that I was showing signs of arthritis due to old age, so you can imagine that I was feeling very depressed by this stage. Being that the bones in my hock had been broken a few months prior to the x-rays being taken, there wasn't much that could be done except to stop riding me. It was the start of a very long holiday for me and it took several months before the swelling finally went away and I was basically sound again, although it was never quite the same after that.

Getting back to my eye, I'm pleased to tell you that my operation went pretty well. They removed the nasty lump and then had to reconstruct my lower eyelid because they had removed a lot of tissue from it. Leanne came to see me as soon as she got the call to say I was out, and I was very groggy when she arrived. My eye had a gauze swab stitched into it to help drain fluid out of the wound and I must have looked awful. I had to stay in the hospital for the night but then the next day I was allowed to go home, thankfully. I'd had enough bad news from that place lately!

Once my stitches were out and my wound was all healed I had to have a series of injections into the eyelid to try to stop the cancer from coming back. While I had been healing, Leanne spoiled me with all my favourite treats. Apples, carrots, pears, bread, sugar cubes, she even shared her packets of chips with me. Everything seemed to have gone well and I was finally getting back on track. I would like to say that this was the last of my experiences with the vet but unfortunately there would be many, many more to come.

Chapter 4 – Memories and mishaps

The season was turning to autumn and the world around me was changing into a cascade of brown and orange leaves, which had turned brittle and fallen from their trees to settle on the ground below. As I walked briskly along the trail I heard the leaves crunching under my feet and skipping across the path ahead, carried along by a refreshing cool breeze. Autumn was a glorious time in Canberra, the days were the perfect temperature and there was barely a cloud in the wide clear blue sky.

I remember breathing the crisp clean air deep into my lungs and shaking my head to get rid of an annoying stray blowfly. There were 4 of us out with our respective owners, and we were setting off on a little adventure. The girls had brought our lead ropes and a backpack, and we were going to a nearby park called Fadden Pines for a picnic. I had been to the pines a few times before and it was a lovely exciting place. The only problem was that in the middle of the forest there was a big playground teeming with kids, and the second they caught sight of a horse there was a stampede of little people running to pat me. It was lucky that I am a quiet old mare because they can be quite frightening. In their excitement they don't realise that running flat-out, waving their arms and screaming 'horsey, horsey!' can actually be very traumatic for us!

Before we went to the pines, we had a detour to make. We rode through the quiet streets of Macarthur, our hooves clip-clopping peacefully on the bitumen as we made our way to the first stop – the local takeaway! The girls wanted to get some hot chips for the picnic, and as we walked I wondered if the takeaway shop sold those yummy horse puddings like the ones Leanne made me on special occasions. I guess they don't because I didn't get one, despite giving Leanne my best most hopeful starving face when we arrived.

When we got to the shop, I was feeling a little nervous because it was a very strange place indeed. People rushed around in all directions carrying noisy plastic bags, there were more cars than I had ever seen in one place before, and everybody was staring at us. I guess they weren't expecting to see 4 horses waiting outside the takeaway when they went to get their lunch that day!

One of the girls went inside and when she came back out she had the chips and two bottles of soft drink. Leanne put all three things into the backpack, the girls mounted and we headed towards the pines across the road. Once we were walking through the forest I started to relax and really enjoy myself. The tall sweet-smelling trees seemed to go on forever, almost reaching up into the clouds with their gnarled old branches. When we reached the clearing where the playground was, I was relieved to see that there wasn't a soul anywhere in sight. We trotted across the green manicured grass and stopped when we reached a cluster of small trees in the middle of the park. The girls dismounted, took our saddles off and tied each of us to one of the trees. Then they sat around in the shade, eating hot chips, drinking their fizzy bubbly drinks, talking and laughing. I grazed for a few minutes and then, feeling tired, I thought I might rest my eyes for a moment. I must have dozed off though because when I woke up the girls had put their rubbish in the bin and were ready to saddle up. As we wandered home we were all feeling very light-hearted; it had been such a nice outing and the weather was absolutely stunning. The girls rode us with loose reins and their feet hanging out of the stirrups all the way home.

Sometimes Leanne reminds me of this happy day we spent together, amongst the trees under the never-ending blue sky. She says that when she's at Fadden Pines she looks at the patch of trees where we had our picnic and it makes her smile.

There is another day we spent together that sticks in my mind, but it wasn't such a pleasant experience. It was the first and only time that Leanne actually entered me in a show. It was a small gymkhana run by the local adult riding club and she thought that it would be fun to take me out and try to win a ribbon or two. She was very excited and for the whole week before the big day she talked about it constantly. She had even borrowed a lovely western bridle for me to wear in my led classes.

The day before the show she brought me into the wash bay and gave me a bath, scrubbing me from ears to tail. It wasn't a very nice bath though, because the weather was turning colder – it was almost winter again. Once she had dried me off with a towel she put my lovely warm rug on in an attempt to keep me clean in case I decided to roll in the dust. I loved my rugs, I hadn't had any for ages until I met Leanne! For the winter she had bought me 2; a soft padded doona rug and a blanket-lined canvas one. At the moment I was only wearing the canvas one occasionally when the nights were very cold.

Anyway, getting back to the show preparation! I was sparkling clean and so was my saddle and bridle, she had spent a long time oiling and polishing and cleaning all of my equipment. Very early the next morning she dragged me from my paddock and onto the truck that was to take me to the show. Unfortunately, it was a horrible grey miserable day and it rained all morning.

When we got to the gymkhana Leanne put me in a yard and went to enter me in a few classes. She ended up deciding to buy a day ticket, which meant that she could take me in any class I was eligible for. I was bored and restless, the rain had made me very bad-tempered, and Leanne was cranky and uncomfortable in her jacket and tie so by the time my first class started neither of us were in a very good mood. It was a led class for coloured breeds, which meant paints, pintos, appaloosas and palominos, and there were only two other horses entering besides me. There was Marty, another appaloosa that lived at Macarthur with me, and there was a tiny fat pinto miniature pony being led by a frumpy woman who looked even crankier than Leanne. The class wasn't difficult by any means. All that we had to do was walk out nicely into the centre of the ring, then trot in a big circle around the outside, then stop and stand still in the middle and present for the judge.

Marty the appaloosa gelding went first and completed the task perfectly. I was to go second, and for the whole time that we had been standing there waiting I had carried on like I was at the mad hatter's tea party. I wouldn't stand still and I tossed my head angrily and chomped against my bit in the rain. Leanne hissed at me to stand up and behave myself but I was beyond caring at that stage. As we headed into the ring for our workout I jogged beside her, refusing to walk. When she tried to slow me down I started to circle around her, snorting and bouncing around like an absolute twit. When we got to the point where we had to trot, I started pig-rooting and bucking and then tried to run out of the ring. Leanne was furious with me and her dark eyes burned into mine as she glared and struggled to control me. We jogged back to the middle of the ring and instead of standing nicely before the judge, I reared and danced on the spot like a cornered brumby. I could sense Leanne's frustration and disappointment as we watched the miniature pony trotting neatly around the ring.

The judge considered her options for a moment and then awarded first place to Marty, second to the tubby little pony, and third place to me. I wouldn't even stand still while she tied the white ribbon around my neck; I was too bothered by the awful weather, and the borrowed bridle I was wearing was hurting me.

Despite the fact that she had paid 20 dollars for a day ticket, Leanne didn't enter me in any more classes that day. I knew that she was embarrassed that a tiny pony had beaten us, and she was mad at me for behaving the way I did. She was a bit of a sore loser and didn't have that competitive streak that you needed to survive in the world of showing. We were both relieved to get home that evening, and Leanne said to me that she didn't need a blue ribbon to prove that she had the best horse in the world. As she brushed me and put my rug on I knew she had forgiven me already.

She still has the white felt ribbon from that day, and she says it's very special to her because we won it together, even if I did get beaten by a 2-foot tall horse!

A few weeks after this disastrous day, the weather began to turn colder and Leanne started putting my nice warm blue canvas rug on me every single night. I had only been wearing it for about a week when I had a very rude and unwelcome visitor very late one night.

I was snoozing happily out in the middle of the paddock, deep in a dream about a tree that never ran out of delicious apples, when I was woken suddenly by a strange noise. I could hear something coming towards me, slowly getting closer, twigs and dead leaves crunching underfoot as a dark shape appeared out of the darkness. I snorted in fear and just as I was about to turn and run away, I heard a voice and realised it was a person walking towards me. The shadowy figure stretched out their hand to me and I smelled the bread before I saw it. I accepted the offering from this mysterious stranger, wondering what they were doing here in the middle of the night. The person put a harsh coarse rope around my neck and I saw that there was a second shadow standing a few metres away. The first stranger held me with the rope as the other person walked up to me, and I was surprised and unhappy when they started to undo my nice warm rug. Once all the straps were undone they pulled it very roughly from my back and immediately I felt the cold tingle of the winter air on my coat.

Now that they had my rug they both became very unfriendly and took the rope from around my neck and hit me with it. I was very frightened and confused and I quickly turned and galloped away into the night. Those unkind people had stolen my rug! I watched from a safe distance as they carried it through the paddock, and there was just enough moonlight for me to see them climbing through the fence and getting into a car that was parked on the side of the road. I didn't sleep a wink for the rest of the night.

Leanne arrived the next morning to take my rug off for the day, and she was very surprised to find me standing there without it. At first she thought that maybe I had gotten it caught on a fence or a tree and ripped it off, so she went for a walk around the whole paddock to look for it. I knew that she wouldn't find it but of course I had no way of telling her this fact. She eventually gave up looking after she found the red surcingle that had been around my belly, which was meant to keep the rug from slipping to one side. It was tossed on the ground on the other side of the fence and when she discovered this she realised that it had been stolen. She was very angry and later that afternoon she found out that several horses in the area had been robbed just like me. She went straight down to the saddlery and bought me a beautiful new rug which was much nicer than the one I had just lost. It was very warm and snug and covered in a tartan pattern which I liked very much!

Before she put it on me, she got a tin of white paint and on one side she painted my name in huge letters. On the other side she painted her surname and her phone number. Then to top it off, she painted 'I KICK' on the tail flap, hoping that this would scare off anyone trying to undo my leg straps. The new rug didn't get stolen but I did accidentally tear it apart a few months later. It was the first of many that I would destroy over the coming years... oops!

Chapter 5 – Sickness and sadness

In the few years since Leanne and I had become friends, I'd had countless amounts of cuts, bites, mysterious ailments and of course my eye cancer and broken hock. But the worst was yet to come and it would almost take away my life.

It was a Saturday morning and Leanne had come to the paddocks to visit me. She came walking down towards me, calling out to me, but instead of whinnying and coming to meet her I just stood there. As she got closer she saw that something was very wrong. I was standing still, all hunched up and looking very distressed. My ears were pinned back, my muzzle was crinkled up with pain and I kept swishing my tail unhappily. I didn't budge when she reached me but I could see that she was very worried, especially when I rejected the carrot that she offered me. She put my halter on and I started to tremble as she tried to get me to walk. Every step I took was agony; it felt like a thousand red hot knives were stabbing me in the belly over and over. She managed to get me to walk, one step at a time, to the yards and by the time we got there I was sweating with pain and exhaustion. I wasn't interested in eating my feed, I just wanted to stand completely still in an attempt to stop the pain that radiated through my body. I had a fever, I felt very hot but I was shaking and covered with a cold sweat. I could hear Leanne beside me on the phone to the vet, talking as she put a light rug over me to stop me getting a chill, but I couldn't concentrate on anything except how much I was hurting. At first she thought that I had colic but I didn't really have the right symptoms. I wasn't biting or kicking at my belly, I wasn't trying to get down and roll, I just had this terrible fiery pain in my belly that I could barely stand.

It seemed like hours before the vet arrived but it was only about 40 minutes. It was my usual vet, and I was very happy to see her because generally she was the one that fixed me when I was broken. After a careful examination she decided it wasn't colic, and decided to do a procedure called a peritoneal tap. This meant that she wanted to get a sample of the fluid inside my belly to see if there was any sign of an infection.

First she shaved a small section of my underbelly, right in the middle, and then she gave me a needle to make it all numb. Once the anaesthetic had kicked in, she took a scalpel and made a small incision, then she took an odd-looking metal thing like a giant needle and with a great deal of pressure she pushed it right through the cut she had just made, into the inside of my tummy. It acted as a drain and as she held a container under it, some of the fluid started to drip out. In a normal healthy horse it should be nice and clear with a pale greenish tinge to it, but mine was nothing like that. It was thick and opaque and yellow and the vet knew immediately what was wrong with me. I had peritonitis. This was a fairly common but serious condition, a nasty infection and inflammation of the inside lining of my belly, and it could be fatal if it wasn't treated properly.

She removed the big metal needle thing from my tummy and put a few stitches in to close the wound. She gave Leanne lots of syringes and needles, and a few bottles of penicillin to give me. Before she left she gave me an injection of painkillers, which I was eternally grateful for. Leanne had been given lots of instructions and the vet told her to ring if she was worried or if I got any worse. I had to stay in one of the yards for the next few days so that Leanne could monitor how much I was eating and keep an eye on how much manure I passed.

That night I didn't get any sleep, the pain was still terrible and I trembled and ached and moved restlessly about all night. Leanne arrived very early the next morning to check on me and give me a needle, and I was in a very bad way. No matter what I did, I couldn't stop the pain in my stomach and I was becoming very depressed indeed. I was still refusing to eat or drink; just the thought of putting food in my belly made me shudder. I couldn't even lie down in that yard because the ground was rock hard dirt and all of my joints were aching.

Leanne decided to take me out onto the grass to see if I would like to try grazing for a while, so once again step by step we walked slowly until we got to a nice shady spot under some wattle trees. The grass was green and juicy-looking but I had no interest in eating it. As soon as we stopped walking I did a quick check for any stray rocks, and finding none I dropped my nose to the ground and laid down. It took all of my energy to lower my poor aching body onto the grass and once I was down I had no idea how I was ever going to get up again. I laid there groaning as the pain continued to shoot right through me and all I could think about was making it stop somehow; I couldn't take it anymore. Leanne sat down beside me and started stroking my face, trying to soothe me, and I was so exhausted and miserable that I just laid right back and rested my head in her lap. I was very sick and my willpower to get better was fading fast.

I lay there for a long time like that, with my dearest friend beside me acting as a very comfortable pillow. I couldn't even open my eyes anymore; it was all too much for an old horse to bear. I sensed that my heart was beginning to slow down; I could hear it thudding in my ears, the beats getting further and further apart. It felt as if I didn't need to breathe as much anymore either and I started to take shallow breaths, the air

rasping in and out of my tired old lungs. This was it…
I was dying.

All this time, Leanne had been watching me very
closely and she stopped patting me when she noticed
the change in my breathing. She sat very still listening to me and watching the rise and fall of my side as
I struggled for breath. She suddenly realised what was
happening – I was giving up. The pain was more than
I could handle and I was letting myself slip away. But
there was no way this girl was going to let her best
friend die and with all of her strength she lifted my
heavy head from her lap and forced me to sit up. Then
she got to her feet and started pulling on my lead
rope, urging me to get up. She was crying, big fat tears
streaming down her distraught face, and she started
yelling at me. 'Don't you dare give up! Don't you dare!
Get up! Stand up!' she cried as she pulled and pulled on
the rope. I had been drifting off, my life slipping away
like grains of sand in the wind, but when she started
yelling the emotion in her voice made that floating
feeling disappear and I was thrown suddenly back
into consciousness. I didn't want to get up, I couldn't
stand the pain I had been in but when I looked at
Leanne and saw how distressed she was, something in
me changed.

It was like a light being switched on. I didn't like seeing her so upset and suddenly I realised what we were
both losing if I gave up and let myself die. I mustered
every ounce of strength I could find and forced myself

to stand up. Once I was on my feet Leanne made me walk around and around, she made me keep moving, keep breathing, and when she had calmed down and put me back in my yard I was feeling much stronger. The power of the mind is an amazing thing, as is the power of friendship, and she willed me to get better that day. I did it for her and over the next few days I improved dramatically and was finally allowed to go back into the paddock with my friends. Looking back now, I'm so glad that I managed to get through it because I would have missed out on so many fantastic years of happiness, and all the great memories that came with them.

A few months after my bout of peritonitis, there was a terrible incident that got everyone at Macarthur talking. Tragically, it was to be the beginning of the end for the horse involved.

Candy was an appaloosa, just like me, except I was grey and she was more of a strawberry roan colour. She hadn't lived with us for very long, and she told me she had come from a riding school near a little town called Wee Jasper. She wasn't a very social horse, she preferred to keep to herself and this was a quick way to make enemies in a herd environment. I should know, I was exactly the same! There was one horse in particular that was always picking on her, a cranky hairy old gelding who seemed to take great pleasure in chasing her away from the water trough, or biting her on the rump as she walked past him. Candy and the grumpy gelding were both very... how shall I put it... 'chubby'... horses, and for this reason they found themselves locked up in the founder paddock together. The founder paddock was very small with no grass in it; I guess you could say it was like the equine equivalent of going on a diet, and the pair of them were to stay in there until they lost some weight.

When Candy had her accident there were no witnesses, but word on the paddock was that her grumpy paddock mate had chased her straight into the fence. All I knew was that one minute they were both in there, and the next time I looked over, Candy was gone. The ringlock boundary fence of the founder paddock had been badly damaged, there were snapped wires sticking out wildly and it was all bent out of shape. A few of Candy's tail hairs still lingered on the barbs of the broken fence, and on the fresh spring breeze we could all smell the warm scent of blood; I remember how nervous that smell made me and I shifted my weight restlessly and snorted, trying to blow it out of my nostrils.

Hours later, Candy was returned to the paddocks. She had been found wandering in a daze down beside the nearby Monaro Highway and she was in a very bad way. Her back legs were torn to shreds and she had lost a great deal of blood. Her owner, Joan, came racing out to Macarthur and we horses all stood in the paddock watching the whirlwind of activity that followed. Shortly after Joan's arrival, the vet turned up and there were all sorts of needles and wound dressings and bandages coming out of the back of her car. Judging by the injuries, the state of the fence and the hoof marks in the ground, it looked as if Candy had indeed been run into the fence. Her legs had become tangled in the wire and in her panic and fright she had flipped herself right over the fence. The wire had basically stripped the flesh from her hind legs and left her cannon bones exposed. It was a horrendous thing to happen to a horse and we all felt terribly sorry for her. Once the vet had done her best to patch Candy up, a truck arrived and they loaded her up and took her away. None of us would see her again for a long time.

Candy had to stay at the vet hospital for several days while they stitched and patched her up, and they even had to put a plaster cast on one of her legs. She had bandages from hoof to belly and she could hardly walk. Then she was moved from the vet hospital to an agistment centre, where she had her own stable to live in while she was healing. It took months and months and it cost poor Joan a great deal of money, but Candy was her special friend and she wanted to do the best she could for her.

By the time that Candy was well enough to come back to Macarthur the season had changed, summer was in full swing and it was extremely hot and dry. She still had some bandages on, so the decision was made to keep her in one of the holding yards for a couple of weeks. It was the best thing to do in her situation; putting her back in with the herd and letting her run around would risk opening up her freshly healed wounds. She had been in the yard for about a week when she started to get sick.

The days had been overwhelmingly hot, the air was dusty and dry and the heat of the sun was relentless. The ground was baked rock hard and Candy had been standing there in that little yard, day after day, until she couldn't handle the heat anymore. There was a large gum tree that provided shade for part of the day but as the sun moved across the sky she would be left with only the harsh summer sunlight. It wasn't long before she was suffering from heatstroke. Unfortunately for her, nobody realised until it was too late.

Leanne was saddling me up one afternoon when she heard a strange sound. When she turned around she saw that Candy had knocked her plastic bin of water over, and she was paddling in the puddle it had created. Leanne stood the bin back up and filled it up again with the hose from the wash bay, but she had barely taken three steps before Candy tipped the bin straight over again. Surprised and a little confused, Leanne told Candy to stop it, and filled the bin up once more. But it was to no avail because once again the overheated horse knocked it over and stood there splashing herself with her front feet. Leanne was getting a bit annoyed by this stage and she filled it up once more before we headed off for our ride. While she had the water on, she sprayed the hose all over Candy to cool her off, and the poor mare seemed to love the feeling of the cold water running down her back and sides. If only Leanne had realised why...

That evening while the yard was busy with the buzz of feeding time, some of the girls noticed the injured mare behaving strangely. She had continued to knock her water over all afternoon, and now she was rolling constantly and biting at her stomach. All the signs pointed to that dreaded word – Colic. Joan was called and she rushed to the paddocks once again to wait for the vet. Everybody was very worried and stayed around to make sure that everything was alright. The vet was there for a long time treating Candy and when she finally left she told Joan that she should start to improve soon and would hopefully be fine. This, however, would not be the case at all.

The next morning the unlucky mare seemed to be a little bit brighter, but as the day wore on she started to go downhill again. When Leanne arrived to feed me that afternoon she was horrified to see that Candy's belly was hugely swollen and as tight as a drum. When she tapped lightly on it, it sounded hollow, and the poor mare was clearly in pain. She rang Joan to let her know, but Joan couldn't get there. She didn't have a driver's licence and her partner who usually drove her around was not home. She asked Leanne if she could wait while she arranged for the vet to come back, which Leanne was more than happy to do. 2 other horse owners, Julianne and Sandy, also waited with her. The vet didn't arrive until very late that evening, when it was almost dark, and by then the poor mare was suffering badly.

Her belly looked like it could burst and the vet could hear fluid moving around in there. The kindly vet explained to Leanne and her friends that because Candy had been so hot in the sunny yard she had developed heatstroke, which then caused an impaction or blockage in her gut. In a cruel twist, the heatstroke had caused Candy to drink lots and lots of water. That water was all trapped in her stomach and couldn't get out, due to the gut blockage, which was why we were now seeing that hugely swollen belly.

The vet carefully inserted a tube into the mare's nostril and fed it down into her belly to drain the liquid out. As soon as the tube was in, the water started pouring out and Candy must have felt relieved by this because she gave a soft, grateful little whinny. It was dark by this stage and the vet shone her torch onto the pool of liquid forming on the ground from the mare's belly. It was slightly red, tinted with blood, and the vet informed the 3 girls that Candy's stomach or gut must have ruptured from the pressure of all the water that had backed up behind the blockage. There were two options; the first was that they could try to operate, but she suspected that it was already too late for that. It was also very expensive and everyone knew that Joan could not possibly afford another vet bill. The second option was the one that they were all dreading – Candy would have to be put down.

By the time the vet said the word 'euthanasia' the girls were already crying. But the worst was yet to come; one of them would have to ring Joan and tell her the awful news – it was her dear friend's last night on earth. Leanne and Julianne were far too upset to talk so Sandy agreed to make the grim call. I remember Leanne saying that she could hear Joan start crying over the phone all the way from where Sandy was standing across the yard talking to her. Sandy had broken the news, and then she passed the phone to the vet so that she could explain everything properly. Joan wanted desperately to be there but her very unkind partner refused to drive her over, even though it was only 10 minutes away, so she never even got to say a proper goodbye.

The girls led Candy over to a secluded spot on the grass; we all watched silently from the paddock as they walked, tears shining on their faces in the moonlight. Leanne and Julianne had never seen a horse being put down before, and they stroked the mare's neck and whispered softly to her as the vet put the first needle in. She injected the green contents of the syringe and quickly swapped it for another full one. She was halfway through injecting the second lot when it took effect and without warning Candy slumped to the ground. She breathed out one last time, a long sad sigh, then she lay still. After all those months of Joan's hard work to heal her wounds, it had taken only seconds for the mare to die. She would feel no more pain now.

Leanne was crying uncontrollably by the time it was all over; it was a terrible thing for a soft-hearted young girl to see. Sandy had called Leanne's mum to come and pick her up, but before she left she took off Candy's halter. She also cut off a piece of her tail and plaited it, to give to Joan as a keepsake. They put a rug over her to try to prevent upsetting anyone that arrived the next morning, and then they all left. There was a quiet sadness lingering across the herd and we all thought the sky seemed much darker than normal that night.

First thing the next morning Joan came to say her goodbyes before the truck came to take Candy's body away. She knelt on the ground beside her beloved unmoving friend and sobbed and sobbed. She placed a small bunch of flowers next to her before she left. Not long after Joan had gone, the truck arrived and they attached chains to the mare's legs to pull her onto the truck. I think the biggest insult of all was that they put the chains on the leg that was still bandaged, tearing it open all over again as she was taken away to be returned to the earth.

The world of horses is not always smiles and sunshine, there are endless things that can go wrong without warning and this incident was just a drop in the ocean. We are very fragile creatures, with awkwardly designed bodies and delicate minds, and sometimes seemingly harmless things can prove to be fatal. Something as simple and beautiful as sunshine created a deadly chain reaction that caused our friend to die and we think of her every time that hot summer wind whispers in our ears.

Chapter 6 – My two different sides

I had generally always been a very quiet mare, usually extremely well-behaved. I didn't buck or rear, I basically never pig-rooted and I especially never tried to bolt. But as Leanne and I got to know each other better and she became more confident and daring, I started to let my hair down a bit. It was Leanne's fault really! She and her friends were always doing crazy things, like going over big jumps bareback with their arms stretched out in the air, not even holding onto the reins. They would ride us down though steep little gullies, jump over watercourses, gallop over big mounds of dirt and all manner of other things!

There was a section of the trail we usually rode on that all the girls called 'bolting hill' because it was a long uphill stretch of grass and it was lovely to gallop up. At first I would just canter leisurely to the top and always be the last to arrive, but one day I decided to kick up my heels. There were 4 or 5 of us out for a ride and I was feeling particularly good that afternoon. I was fat and round from the sweet spring grass, the sun was shining and I was very fit and healthy. As we approached bolting hill we all broke into a trot, and as the others started to canter I put my head down and attempted my best almighty buck! I knew that Leanne would try to rein me in, which she did, so I danced around on the spot, fighting the bit and swishing my tail in frustration. I knew Leanne was very surprised at my naughty behaviour but she knew what I wanted so after a few seconds she turned me towards the top of the hill and let me have my head. I lunged forward into a gallop and we thundered along, leaving a trail of dust as my hooves kicked up the sandy soil. Everybody else was already at the top and they sat there staring at me in shock as I raced towards them. They had never seen me galloping, I was usually so slow! By the time we reached the top of the hill I was very tired but I hadn't felt so alive in ages!

A few weeks later as Leanne saddled me up, I was in a very silly mood; it was quite windy and that always stirred me up and made me very nervous. Don't ask me why, it's just a horse thing. Everything is spookier and more likely to try to eat us on a windy day, ask any horse and they will tell you! Anyway, getting back to the story, Leanne had mounted and was trying to get me to walk down the driveway towards the gate. I didn't want to go and I was carrying on like mad, dancing around and tossing my head, snorting and shying at things that weren't even there. In the end Leanne was so fed up with me that she dismounted and started to lead me. As she dragged me towards the gate I shied again, and ran forward suddenly. She had been walking in front of me and as I jumped forward, the toe of my front hoof hit the back of her leg. As I put my weight onto that foot, it slid right down along the back of her calf and her Achilles tendon. She cried out in pain and pulled on the reins to move me away from her, making me throw my head in the air in protest and run backwards a few steps. She yelled at me to 'stand up, you idiot!' so I knew she was really cranky, and then she pulled up the leg of her jeans to see what damage I had done to the back of her ankle. It was all red and purple, starting to swell, and there was a nasty graze all the way down her leg. The back of her shoe was crushed and I could see that she was in a lot of pain. But she was so stubborn and so angry with me for being that silly over nothing that she climbed onto my back and forced me out of the gate onto the trail. She was nearly crying and she had the injured foot hanging down out of the stirrup, because it was too painful to move it.

I knew I was in trouble now so I did as I was told and walked along very quietly for the whole ride, ignoring the invisible gremlins that lurked behind every tree as it blew in the wind. By the time we got back, her ankle was horribly swollen and she couldn't move it or put any weight on it. She could hardly undo her shoelace from the swelling and it was turning very black and bruised. I felt guilty for hurting her but as always, I had no way of telling her that.

She went home that night very upset with me, and the next day when she arrived to feed me she was on crutches, with her ankle all bandaged up. She told me that she'd had to go to the hospital for x-rays but luckily it wasn't broken. The tendon had been injured and she was very upset because her school formal was only a couple of weeks away. Fortunately, she was able to walk without her crutches by the time the big night came along but she still had some terrible bruising. Now whenever she is leading me and I am being naughty she walks beside me, rather than in front of me. I guess sometimes the only way to learn these things is the hard way.

Despite a few little incidents like these, I was still generally very quiet. I swear, I was! Leanne had even taught a friend of hers how to ride on me, and that girl now had a pony of her own. But there was one day in particular when I was feeling very cheeky and rebellious and I just couldn't stop myself from being naughty. We were in paddock number 5 at Macarthur, and to get to it you had to walk through one of the other paddocks. Usually to save walking all the way back, Leanne would jump on me bareback and ride me up to the yards, and we would have a lovely canter up the hill on the way. But on this day when she came to catch me, she had somebody with her. The girl's name was Sharon and she was Leanne's stepcousin. Sharon said that she knew how to ride and she wanted to hop on and ride me to the yards instead of Leanne. As she climbed awkwardly onto my back, I heard Leanne telling her that if I started to trot she'd better pull me back to a walk straight away, otherwise I would run all the way to the top of the hill. Sharon mustn't have been paying attention though, as I would soon find out. Heehee!

We started walking down through the paddock and I could sense that Sharon was nervous and not actually very confident at all. That devilish feeling rose up in me and I couldn't help myself, it was too tempting. I began to walk faster and as we got to the place where the uphill slope started, I broke into a trot. I could hear Leanne yelling out to make me walk, but Sharon was too busy to pay attention; she was trying not to bounce right off my back as I jogged along. I knew she had lost control of me so I snorted with glee, tossed my head and leapt forward into a very fast canter. If horses could laugh, I would have been giggling like a cheeky hyena. I surged on up the hill and Sharon screamed and screamed all the way up, holding onto my cotton rug for dear life. I was surprised that although she bounced around like a sack of potatoes, she didn't fall off.

We reached the fence at the yards and I came to a sudden stop. Leanne was running up the hill behind me yelling out at Sharon to jump off while I was standing still. But the silly girl didn't get off so I decided to go for another little run. I turned and started cantering along the fence line, then changed direction and headed for the gate leading into the founder paddock. Through the narrow gateway we went, with the strange girl screeching like a monkey the whole way. I was having a lovely time amusing myself with this game! But it quickly came to an end a moment later when Sharon finally decided to bail out, and jumped off my back. Then Leanne came running through the gate to grab me and she scolded me all the way back to the yards. I didn't really care though, I was feeling very tough and defiant and I still got fed so it didn't matter. For some reason Leanne stopped telling people I was great with beginners after that!

She got her revenge on me for all of my naughtiness in the end though. The local adult riding club was once again having their autumn gymkhana, and Leanne volunteered to be a runner. This meant that we rode around all day between all of the show rings, collecting results from the judges and taking them to the announcer, we collected dressage tests, and we delivered various messages and things to the stewards. We had done it a few times before and I had to admit it was sort of fun. This particular show, however, would be just a little bit different for me.

The day before the show, Leanne gave me a bath and made sure all of my gear was nice and clean. She seemed to spend a long time getting my tail clean and tangle-free, and I found out why the next morning. She arrived bright and early, with a big silly grin on her face and a spray can in her hand. She had me tied up in the yard, and she was standing behind me playing with my tail. At first I didn't really pay any attention to what she was doing; I was more interested in my breakfast. But then I heard the hissing sound of an aerosol can being sprayed and I quickly turned to see what she was doing.

I was horrified to discover that the spray can she had been holding contained bright pink hair colour, and she was spraying it all over my poor white tail! I snorted in surprise and tried to swish my tail out of her hand, but it was no use. In no time at all the whole thing was hot pink, and she moved onto my mane. I stood there with my ears pinned back in a very disapproving manner, snorting and stomping my foot unhappily on the ground. Once she had finished colouring my mane, I looked like some kind of ridiculous punk pony princess. But she wasn't finished yet!

Just when I thought things couldn't possibly get any worse, I found that she had made two templates out of cardboard; one was a star, and one was a heart. She used one on my face, to give me a pink love heart right in the middle of my head. She used the other to give me some little pink stars scattered over my rump. Now instead of a punk I looked like some sort of pretentious care bear. I couldn't believe she was doing this to me!

When we got to the show I hoped desperately that we wouldn't run into anyone I knew. I was so embarrassed! But everybody seemed to love my daring new hair style, and all day people came up to pat me and comment on how much they loved it. I even had my photo taken by complete strangers a few times, and by the time we went home I didn't feel so bad anymore. The colour gradually faded out after a few days in the sun, and I was back to my normal horse-coloured self! It was typical of Leanne to do these silly things just for fun and now I look back on days like that, shake my head and laugh at the crazy things we used to do together. And like I said earlier, she definitely got her revenge on me for my bad behaviour!

Chapter 7 - New arrivals

In 2002, shortly before Leanne's 18th birthday, I was very unhappy- outraged actually- when I learned that her parents had agreed to let her get another horse. I was jealous! She was my bestest special friend, I didn't want to share her with some cow-hocked buck-toothed nag that would try to steal her from me!

On the day of her birthday I was feeling very stressed and anxious, wondering when the dreaded new intruder would arrive. But the day passed by and when Leanne came to feed me, she told me that her parents had given her an IOU because she hadn't found another horse yet. It took another 2 weeks before a truck pulled in through the gates and parked in front of the yards. I watched with mixed emotions of irritation, anxiety and curiosity as the tailgate was lowered, and then Leanne's new horse came walking slowly down the ramp. I snorted with amusement and surprise when I saw him. What on earth was that thing?!

He was huge, at least 17 hands, with massive hooves the size of dinner plates. His thick haystack of a mane hung down halfway to his knees, and his legs were covered in very long fluffy white hair from the knee down. I knew what this was... It was a clydesdale! I had heard of them but I had never seen one in real life before! The entire herd was now standing at the fence staring and snorting in surprise at this odd-looking newcomer as he was led into one of the holding yards. He was very different to any horse I had seen before but I had to admit he was rather lovely. He had a big white blaze right down the front of his enormous head and under his sweeping forelock he had very friendly and gentle big brown eyes. He stood in his yard looking at us, tall and magnificent, and I suddenly didn't feel jealous anymore. I had a feeling that I would like being friends with this horse. His registered name was Dakota Sam, but his previous owner had called him Moppy. I thought that name suited him perfectly because of his mop-like mess of hair!

Later that afternoon Leanne turned up with a plastic bag in her hand. Inside it was a new halter for Moppy (his head was too big to fit any of my old ones!) and some worming paste. It was paddock regulation that any new horse had to be drenched 24 hours before they went in with the herd. Leanne put the oversized new halter on her new friend and took the drench out of its cardboard box. Up until this point, Moppy had been standing quietly beside her, but upon seeing the wormer he suddenly became very animated! He threw his head high up into the air and charged forward, almost running right over poor Leanne as she tried to settle him down. She stroked his face and talked to him gently but the second she tried to get that wormer near his mouth he would do the same thing, throwing his head up high out of her reach. She gave up trying to hold his lead rope and instead took the side of his halter in her hand. She held it as tight as she could and gave it another go, and this time when he raised his head, he lifted her clean off the ground. She dangled in the air for a second and then let go and dropped back onto the dirt. Her 50-kilogram frame was no match for this massive chunk of horse! Leanne's mother was there watching and by this point she was laughing hysterically at her poor daughter's failed attempts to worm the enormous horse. I had to admit it was very funny and I did have a bit of a giggle to myself while I ate my dinner.

It took about 2 hours to successfully get the drench into Moppy's mouth and by the time it was done, Leanne was very tired and cranky. The next day he was allowed to go out into the paddock with us, and the poor slow-moving gelding copped it from the other horses worse than I did when I was new. He walked as if he was moving in slow motion, he was very dopey, and his reflexes didn't allow him to get out of the way quick enough when he was being attacked. Some of the horses were frightened of him and ran away if he went near them. But one of them, a thoroughbred named BJ, took an instant dislike to him.

I don't know if it was because he was different or because he was an easy target, but BJ made poor Moppy's life hell. No matter where the enormous new gelding went, BJ would be there chasing him, biting him, kicking him, and making him feel very unwelcome. I felt so sorry for him but I was too terrified of BJ to try helping him. The worst thing that nasty thoroughbred did was refuse to let Moppy drink from the only water trough in the paddock. Whenever Mop thought that BJ had gone and it was safe to get a drink, he would come charging out of nowhere to chase him off. In the end Leanne had to escort Moppy to the water trough and protect him while he drank, which meant that for the first few days she was coming up to the paddocks 3 or 4 times a day. Eventually, like the rest of us, he settled in but because he didn't seem to know how to defend himself he was always lowest in the pecking order. Once I got to know him I found that I quite liked him. He was a gentle giant and he spoke with a funny Scottish accent, which he told me was because his clydesdale family traced back to a quaint little town in the heart of Scotland. I giggled to myself when he said this, because an image of him dancing around in a tartan kilt popped into my head. He was a very nice gelding indeed and in the end I was glad that Leanne had chosen him to join our little family.

There were always horses coming and going at Macarthur, and on one particular day a flighty little bay mare arrived. She was an arab, and she may have been quite pretty but she was also quite insane. Some arabs can be a little nutty at the best of times but this one was something else entirely. She would spook in the paddock for no good reason and go bolting off bucking and snorting, she was always jumpy and she never seemed to be able to stand still. She only lived with us for a few short days before something awful happened that left everyone at the paddocks in shock.

It was a fine day, not too cool and not too hot - the perfect weather for exercising a horse. Kerry, the lady who owned the little arab, arrived at Macarthur just before noon. She got her gear out of the car and then caught the new mare and brought her into the yard. She gave her a brush, picked out her feet, and then clipped a lunging rein onto her halter and led her over to the arena.

The mare walked with a lively spring in her step and looked the picture of health; her coat was a lovely rich reddish brown colour and she shone beautifully in the sunlight. Her eyes were bright, her hooves neatly trimmed, and she was in perfect condition. Kerry walked her through the sand on the arena until they reached the middle, and then she began lunging her. The mare didn't seem to want to cooperate and she pranced and snorted and danced about, fighting against the lunge rein and tossing her head. She did a few awkward circles around Kerry, and then it was as if something in her exploded.

One minute she was trotting along, and the next she was completely out of control. She gave a loud high-pitched squeal and reared up angrily, striking out with her front feet. As she reared she looked wild and furious, like a beautiful untamed brumby. Violently she threw her head back, and with that one sudden movement everything went quiet.

It seemed to happen in slow motion. The rear, the movement as her neat little hooves struck out at the air in front of her, her head moving back as she called out, it was all in a split second but as we watched in horror it seemed to take forever. As she stood straight up on her hind legs, the squeal coming from her throat suddenly stopped, and without warning the pretty little mare collapsed.

She was dead before she hit the ground. Her body hit the sand with a thud and she lay perfectly still; her eyes that had been so bright just seconds before now stared blankly into space. For these few surreal seconds everything had gone eerily quiet, but then the silence was broken by Kerry's screams. Over and over she screamed, terrifying and blood-curdling, as she stood on the arena staring in disbelief at the dead horse.

There was blood coming from the mare's nose now, trickling out and staining the sand around her scarlet red. I remember the chill that radiated through me, echoing down my spine as if death itself was touching me with its icy fingers. I snorted in fear, took a few steps back, and then turned and galloped off into the paddock. I ran all the way to the back fence, I had to get away from that horrid scene that had just unfolded. When I went back up to the yards late that afternoon, the little horse's body was gone and Kerry's husband had covered up the blood-stained sand. It seemed strange, there was no sign that the lovely little mare had ever even existed here.

I heard in the paddock a few days later that the vet suspected the mare died from something called an aortic aneurysm. Sometimes the aorta, which is the big artery that carries blood from the heart to the rest of the body, can have a weak spot and when it is under a lot of pressure it can burst, kind of like a tyre that has too much air in it. The vet thought that the little mare must have had a weakened aorta, which was impossible for anyone to know about, and the pressure on her heart when she got angry and reared up caused the weak spot to rupture. She had died instantly when that happened; the only blessing was that she had not felt any pain.

The freak accident left both the equine and human community of Macarthur Park deeply disturbed and upset for quite some time. As you can see, I have a very bittersweet collection of memories from my time living there, but life experiences are the things that make us who we are. I now have a much greater appreciation for how fragile life is, and I will never take it for granted.

Chapter 8 – The day the sky turned red

It was midway through January in 2003 and so far the summer had been relentlessly hot and dry. There was an irritating army of blowflies constantly buzzing around, and there was nearly always a queue to get to the water trough for a refreshing cool drink. For several days I had been able to smell smoke in the air and on this particular Friday night I discovered that there was a bushfire headed our way.

Leanne had already fed me and returned home hours earlier, and I was standing out in the night air dozing and wishing it wasn't so stiflingly hot and muggy. The pungent smell of smoke seemed to be getting stronger so I opened my eyes and looked around for any sign of a fire nearby. I couldn't see anything so I started walking up over the hill to check the yards. When I got to the wooden log fence and looked out into the distance my heart skipped a beat.

Usually one of the nicest things about the Macarthur paddocks was the view from the holding yards. It looked out over the suburbs of Gilmore, Chisholm, Richardson and Calwell, which all sat before the stunning mountainous backdrop of the Brindabella Ranges. On any other day it was picturesque and beautiful, but tonight the sight of it made my mane stand on end. Creeping over the crest of the mountains like lava was an angry, glowing bushfire and although I didn't realise it yet, that fire would prove to be terrifyingly unstoppable.

At the very same moment that I was gazing, wide-eyed and frightened, at the burning mountains, Leanne was doing the same thing from the car park of a nearby restaurant where she had been having dinner. The late night air was still surprisingly warm and laced thickly with the smell of burning eucalypts. Neither of us realised what the following day would bring, and even if we had known, there was nothing anyone could have done to stop it.

When the sun came up the next morning it was a Saturday, and Leanne headed off to the large animals veterinary hospital she worked at, over on the other side of Canberra. She worked there as a stable hand and vet nurse and on that day there weren't many horses being treated at the clinic. By mid-morning all of her patients had been fed and watered, medicated, their stables were clean and she was sweeping spilled hay and sawdust out of the breezeway. Outside, there was an enormous plume of thick grey smoke rising into the air and it was frightfully hot and windy. She always listened to the radio while she was working because generally on weekends she was the only one there and it was very quiet. Today the radio was alive with news updates about the bushfire, which had gotten significantly closer to the suburbs of Canberra overnight.

Just after lunch, they began to sound an alarm over the airwaves, and were instructing people in certain areas to evacuate their homes as the fire was expected to hit at any time. The radio announcer also mentioned that there were dozens, maybe hundreds, of horses currently agisted in the area where the fire was headed. Leanne suspected that there would probably be horses arriving later in the day suffering from burns, or injuries from running through fences trying to escape the blaze. She decided to make sure that every available stable was clean and ready to go, and she filled up every bucket with fresh water, mixed up several feeds and put a biscuit of hay in each stall too.

By about 3 o'clock Leanne decided she couldn't stay at work any longer. The wind was roaring furiously through the trees, and it was so hot and dry that it seemed to suck all the moisture right out of the air. The smoke was so thick that it was hard to breathe and it was blocking out the sun, making it seem as if it was late in the evening rather than bright mid-afternoon. There was nothing more to be done at the clinic so Leanne got in her car and started driving home. I remember her telling me that as she travelled down a road called Erindale Drive, she looked with stunned disbelief at the scene unfolding through her windscreen.

It was even darker now, as if it was midnight, and the sky was an eerie deep red colour. The Brindabella Ranges that had always provided such a pleasant backdrop to the Tuggeranong Valley were now glowing a deep menacing orange, almost red, completely engulfed by the intensely raging bushfire. Burning leaves and embers rained from the sky and all along the roadside people had stopped their cars and were staring or taking photos of the incredible, unrecognisable landscape. Leanne had said it looked like it was the end of the world; a horrible fiery apocalypse.

Leanne continued on to her house, checked that everything was alright there with her parents, and then she came straight up to the paddocks to see what the plan was if we needed to be evacuated. Every horse's owner was there, and each one of us was caught and tied up in the yards for the time being. We were all very afraid and stood restlessly shifting our weight from hoof to hoof, swishing our tails impatiently and snorting at the hot wind filling our nostrils.

All of the owners were huddled around Leanne's little Subaru Brumby ute listening to the radio, and a man's voice was saying that several homes in the suburb of Duffy were alight. Shortly after that, the man who managed the Macarthur paddocks turned up. He got out of his car long enough to tell everyone to leave all the horses in the yards, then he was gone. Nobody was very happy with this and a group decision was made to open all the internal gates of Macarthur Park and let us out into the paddocks. That way if the fire reached us we would have somewhere to run rather than being locked in a small yard with no escape.

That night Leanne and some of the other owners took it in turns coming up every hour to check on us and keep an eye out for spot fires. Fortunately the blaze never got to us, but it caused a horrible amount of destruction throughout Canberra. Over 500 homes were destroyed, 4 people died and countless animals, including many horses, were killed.

When Leanne got to work the next day she was surprised to discover that no injured horses had been brought in to the hospital overnight. It seemed as if any poor beast that was close enough to the fire to sustain an injury had died at the time or been put down at the scene afterwards. The vets had been working around the clock and were very stressed and upset at the loss of life.

Leanne told me a few days later about one of her friends, Julianne, who had kept her horse at an equestrian centre in the suburb of Chapman. Her horse was only 3 years old, a lovely young grey arab named Zoomy, and he had sadly lost his life in the huge fire. Julianne had been staying in Sydney for the weekend and her dad had tried very hard to rescue Zoomy for her. Unfortunately by the time he got there the inferno had hit and he was forced to abandon his rescue attempt and take shelter with dozens of other terrified people in the indoor arena; everybody inside feared for their lives and were almost unable to breathe from the stifling heat of the roaring blaze outside.

The fire eventually passed and the frightened people slowly walked out to a sickening sight; a blackened landscape of charred trees, destroyed buildings and many of their beloved horses burnt to death or suffocated from the heat and smoke. The worst part for poor Julianne's dad was when he had to tell her the devastating news, that he had been unable to save poor young Zoomy, who had still been locked in his stable when the fire hit. He didn't have the heart to tell her the truth while she was away in Sydney with her friends; in an act of kindness he told her a well-intentioned lie over the phone, that he had been able to get to Zoomy in time. It wasn't until she returned home from her trip that he was faced with telling her the heartbreaking truth about her beautiful dapple-grey friend who had perished in the fire. Vale Zoomy.

We at Macarthur Park were very lucky to escape the inferno now known as the infamous 2003 bushfires, but many weren't so fortunate and I would like to dedicate this chapter to the memory of all our equine

friends who were sadly lost on that fateful day, Saturday the 18th of January 2003.

Chapter 9 – Home is a haven

Over the years I had come to love the peace and quiet and rolling green hills of Macarthur paddocks. Sadly, the people who were supposed to be responsible for maintaining things were very neglectful and as time went by the place started to deteriorate; quite frankly the paddocks were becoming more than a little dangerous.

The pasture had grown thick with thistles, capeweed and Paterson's curse, the dams had turned stagnant and scummy, and the fences were in desperate need of repairs. There were loose strands of rusty old barbed wire lying hidden in the grass, waiting to wrap around our legs and cut us to ribbons. Randomly placed star pickets stuck out at odd angles in some of the paddocks, and the yards were looking old and tired. I guess none of us were really surprised the day we got the news that Macarthur Park was being closed down. All of the horse owners were very sad to think that the happy little community they had formed would be breaking apart, with everybody going their separate ways. I hadn't really been too worried about it until I discovered that Leanne was moving me down the trail to the Rose Cottage complex.

Rose Cottage was only a 10-minute ride away but to me it was a whole different world. The horses from there sometimes rode past our fences and many of them were quite nasty, pinning their ears back and snorting rudely at us as they walked by. It did have one of the best work areas in town though, with an arena, polocrosse goals, lots of jumps and plenty of flat space to gallop on. But that was the last thing on my mind; I was thinking about what had happened to poor old Tex.

Tex was a handsome Thoroughbred gelding who had lived at Rose Cottage for several years. We would see him occasionally and give him a friendly nod as we rode by. He was always so nice and cheerful, and we were shocked the day we got the terrible news - Tex had been shot.

It started as a whisper in the paddock one morning, a quiet rumour that no one really believed. But as the day progressed and we heard more and more people talking about it, we knew it was true. He really had been shot! Questions raced through my mind as we waited to hear more updates – how did this happen? Was he alive? Who shot him? It wasn't until late that afternoon that we finally got some answers.

Tex had indeed been shot, but he was alive and he

was going to be fine. Thank goodness for that! His owner had come to visit him that morning, and she had found him in his paddock with a perfectly round hole in his head, just above his eye. She had suspected it was a bullet hole, and when the vet came out they confirmed it. The whole thing was going to be broadcast on television too, because the crew of a show called Animal Hospital were in town and they turned up with the vet to get in on the action! The vet said that Tex was very lucky, because if the bullet had gone in just a couple of centimetres further it could have killed him.

We were all very relieved to hear that he was going to be alright, but the whole incident made us very nervous because they still didn't know who had shot him, or why. The police said that it was probably an accident, that maybe someone had been trying to shoot a kangaroo without realising there were horses around. I wasn't buying that story! For the next few weeks our little herd stayed close together, listening carefully for any strange sounds and keeping watch for people creeping through our paddocks late at night. We never saw anybody, and we also never saw Tex again. His owner was very distressed and moved him to a new home straight away. I don't know where he ended up but I hope that he was happy wherever he was.

Tex's story had haunted me from the moment I first heard about it, and when Leanne told me I would be moving to the place where it had happened, my heart started racing. I was terrified that the shooter might come back! Maybe I would stand out, with my funny mix of colours and the spots all over my rump, and they would target me next time! For several days I worried about it, but of course nothing ever happened. Leanne moved Moppy and I to Rose Cottage, and it actually turned out to be rather nice. There was lots of grass to eat, and poor old Mop always stayed close to me so we could look after each other. Not that he was any good if someone was picking on me, he was the biggest sook I had ever met and he would either hide behind me or run away, even though he was by far the biggest and heaviest horse in the paddock.

We only ended up staying at Rose Cottage for a few months. One day as Leanne was leading me across the carpark, she noticed that I was being quite clumsy and stumbling a lot. I didn't know why but I just hadn't been feeling all that well and sometimes it was hard for me to put my hooves where I wanted them to go. I felt very uncoordinated and Leanne started to get concerned, with good reason. A few days earlier, a pony from my paddock had been moved away after its owner discovered it had liver damage from eating Paterson's curse. One of the possible symptoms was neurological impairment - unsteadiness and loss of coordination- so Leanne arranged for the vet to come out and take a blood sample from me for testing.

A couple of days later the results were in – I was showing early signs of liver damage and would need to be moved to pasture that was free of the dreaded curse. It took Leanne quite a few days to find new agistment for Moppy and I but finally she was offered a large paddock at a lovely complex known as LYH. The manager, Barry, was a very friendly and understanding man and he kindly offered to help after he was told about the Paterson's curse dilemma. The following weekend a truck arrived to pick us up and we were off to our new home. It was only a short drive, and when we got there I was excited to discover that we had a whole huge paddock all to ourselves. No more public agistment, no more getting bitten on the bum by unkind strangers while I was having a drink, no more getting chased away from the gate while I was waiting for Leanne! Hooray! I went galloping madly down to the back of the paddock and kicked and bucked and rolled, delighted with my new surroundings. A couple of minutes later, Moppy appeared, trotting lazily through the grass. He was never in much of a rush to go anywhere. I snorted with amusement at his big cumbersome frame and then went to graze beside him as the sun went down behind us. Moppy's familiar face with his big rubbery lips and friendly gentle eyes closing slowly as he chewed on the green grass was comforting to me. I sighed happily... What a wonderful day.

Once we had settled in for a few days, Leanne saddled me up and we went to explore LYH. It was a lovely place, even though it was riddled with blackened scars where the bushfires had ripped through it the year before. Several buildings on the property had been burnt down, including the stable block, and the hills that surrounded the rolling paddocks were still bare and brittle looking, littered with the skeletons of charred gum trees. Still, it had a peaceful feel about it and I was very happy.

As we came around the corner near the main office, a pretty petite blonde girl on a stunning chestnut gelding came into view. She rode up to us and started talking to Leanne while I stood quietly, feeling shy and awkward in front of the good-looking big gelding. His name was Jake, and he sure was handsome! He danced and pranced and showed off while his rider, Kaz, did her best to settle him down as she chatted. It turned out that she and Leanne had gone to the same college! The girls arranged to go for a ride together the next day and soon after that they became great friends.

The next few months were a blur of happy times, great trail rides and lots of laughter. Jake and I never knew what to expect from Kaz and Leanne but it was always a lot of fun! I remember one day when it was particularly hot and sunny, and the girls decided to take us for a dip in one of the dams near my paddock. It had been a couple of years since Leanne had taken me swimming and I was delighted to stand in the shallows and splash the cool water with my front hoof. It was so refreshing that I would dunk my whole head under, then pull it out and snort and shake the water from my ears. As I did so, my whole body shook too and Leanne would squeal and shout with laughter as she held onto my mane for dear life. Jake was splashing too, and it was showering me with smelly muddy dam water. I couldn't have been happier! And apparently, either could the girls because they were laughing so hard they really had no control over us. Jake went charging forward into the deeper middle of the dam, with Kaz giggling hopelessly on his back. Leanne turned me towards the middle and urged me forward and we all got well and truly soaked as we splashed at the lovely cold water. Several times Jake tried to get down on his knees and have a roll, obviously forgetting about poor Kaz on his back, and she would yell and pull his head up and try to keep him on his feet. Leanne thought this was hilarious and as we stood there watching Jake and Kaz's antics, her laughter echoed right through me and I remember thinking to myself that I would always remember this moment. Days like those were so dear to me. I never would have thought little old spotty me could become the centre of someone's whole world, or that I would be lucky enough to spend my days as I grew older enjoying the blue skies and sunny days with my bestest friend in the world. I keep the memories of that happy afternoon, and many others, tucked safely away in my heart and I often fall asleep at night and dream about them.

I have another memory from those days that always makes me snort with laughter! It was once again a hot summer afternoon and I was standing in the shade, swishing my tail at the buzzing flies and dozing contentedly when I heard the sound of Leanne and Kaz's voices floating up from over near the office building. I lifted my head lazily to see what they were up to, and saw that Barry had given them his ride-on lawnmower so they could cut the grass around the office and toilet block area for him. Well this should be entertaining, I giggled to myself and wandered over to stand at the gate and watch.

The pair of them had no idea what they were doing and within minutes the girls were in hysterics, with both of them perched up on the mower laughing so much they had tears running down their faces. They were trying to drive the mower up a small hill and because the grass was slightly wet the wheels were spinning wildly under the weight of them, sending big blobs of mud flying out behind them. The motor was revving loudly and every so often the tyres would grab and the mower would lurch forward suddenly, causing the giggling pair to squeal in terror and then laugh even harder. By the time they had finished mowing (if you can call it that!) the grass was covered in mud and there were tyre tracks everywhere where they had spun the wheels up the hills and done wild doughnuts on the flat areas. Barry never asked them to mow for him again after that. I can't imagine why...

As the feed in the paddocks died down, Barry would graze his cattle on the edges of the road that ran alongside LYH. He always needed horses and riders to help keep them in line, and sometimes when Leanne wasn't working she would saddle me up and we'd spend the day out in the sunshine watching the cows and calves as they munched hungrily on the green grass at the roadside.

Leanne soon realised that I had worked cattle before, when we were pushing them down the road and a cheeky steer ran onto the bitumen. I instantly jumped sideways and headed it off, pinning my ears back, baring my teeth and chasing it back into the herd. She was surprised and very pleased with me and she clapped me on the neck proudly as the cattle continued on ahead. Some people might have found it boring to sit on a horse staring at grazing cows for hours on end but Leanne and I always loved it. Whether we were taking them up to the hill behind the property or guiding traffic carefully through the herd along the road, it was always fun. Sometimes Leanne would bring a backpack filled with water bottles and some lunch for herself, and she would pack me some carrots, or occasionally an apple or even a pear!

One day Leanne arrived early in the morning to visit

me. I could see her from where I stood in my paddock, with her ute parked on the edge of the road talking to Barry. After a few minutes she came driving up to the gate and I whinnied a greeting and came wandering down to see what treats she might have to offer me. I could sense immediately that something was wrong; she looked very concerned and seemed distracted and anxious. As she straightened my rug and checked my legs she began telling me that several horses in the area had become very ill from Paterson's curse, the very plant that we had moved here to avoid. Although Barry took great care to spray as much of the property as he could, there was still quite a lot of the noxious weed growing throughout some of the paddocks. There was a theory getting around that the intense heat of the bushfires may have caused the Paterson's curse to become far more toxic than it normally would be, but no one seemed to know for sure.

Over the next couple of weeks, things took a turn for the worse. Some of the horses who had become ill started to die, and in a most unpleasant way at that. There was one grey gelding who had been sick for a few days, and one night the effects of the toxic plant became too much and he seemed to lose control of himself. He went mad in his paddock and sent himself crashing through the fence in the middle of the night, tearing off down the road cut and bleeding from the wire. The worst part was that the next morning somebody found him all tangled up hanging in the fence at the front entrance to LYH. He was in a very bad way and a vet had to come straight out to put him down. It really was terrible.

Day after day when Leanne would come to feed me, there would be stories filtering through that another horse had passed away or been put down. Leanne organised for one of the vets to take a blood sample from me to be tested, to make sure that I wasn't affected. She wasn't really worried though, because I was looking like a million bucks! My sleek summer coat was smooth and shining, I was very fit and had excellent muscle tone from all the riding we were doing, I was eating well and looked better than I had in years (if I don't say so myself!). That's why when the test came back with a very bad result you could have knocked Leanne over with a feather, she was so shocked.

A normal result for an equine liver function test or GGT (that stands for Gamma Glutamyl Transferase) is generally somewhere between 20 and 50. My test had come back with a horrifying reading of 499. Leanne was very surprised and so was I, although I had been feeling quite tired and run down lately. The most frightening thing was that there were horses on the property that had been so sick they'd been euthanized with levels only half as high as mine. Was I only a matter of days away from the end of my life? I felt the hairs in my mane standing on end and a cold shiver ran down my spine. So many horses had passed away that Barry had needed to hire big machines to dig a large hole to bury them all in, rest their souls, and the thought of ending up in there made me feel sick to my stomach. How could this be happening to me?

Leanne had been given the test results from the receptionist at the vet, and because they were so busy (hundreds of horses across the ACT were being tested and falling ill) it took another 2 days for the vet to ring her to discuss what the result meant. While she was waiting, she went with her mum to talk to Barry and get his opinion on what she should do.

He was very concerned about how high my reading was, and suggested to Leanne that there was a strong possibility that the damage to my liver would be too bad and I may need to be put down. Leanne broke down in tears right there in his lounge room, and her mum started to cry too because she knew how destroyed Leanne would be if she lost me. After a long nervous wait the vet finally called, and in light of the fact that I wasn't showing any obvious symptoms of being sick and was looking so healthy they suggested that I be immediately taken off any pasture, be locked up in a yard and put on an extremely low protein diet. This would take the pressure off my liver by lessening the load of nutrients it had to process.

By the end of that day, I was confined to a small dirt yard which Leanne covered with a layer of comfy sawdust for me lie in. My yummy usual food was replaced with a bland mix of boring oaten chaff and tasteless low-fat pellets. No more lucerne hay for me either, but I was allowed to have meadow hay so Leanne had a lovely big round bale delivered to the yard just for me. I remember her saying that as I stood there tucking into the enormous roll of hay she could almost feel the happiness radiating from me, I was so pleased to have so much food all to myself!

Days in my little yard turned into weeks, and weeks eventually turned into months as I slowly recovered with the help of my boring but necessary restricted diet. Leanne was putting a special Vitamin B supplement into my feed to help my liver regenerate itself. Along with that she also tipped a capful of very stinky seaweed extract liquid in my dinner every night, and finally she had put white clay into my drinking water and squished it between her fingers every day until the water was milky and white. Many people at LYH had started doing this, as the clay was supposed to help purify the body and remove toxins.

I don't know whether it was just one of these things or a combination of all of them, or maybe it was sheer good luck, but by some miracle when I had another blood test a few months later, my GGT was back within the normal range. With absolutely no logical explanation, the baffled vet declared that I had completely recovered.

Chapter 10 – Indoors outdoors

The bushfires of 2003, as I mentioned earlier, had destroyed the stables at LYH. Throughout the months that I had spent recovering in my little yard, plans had been drawn up and work had begun on building 2 brand new stable blocks on the site of the old ones. They were to be the same design as the ones used in the Sydney 2000 Olympics, and I was very excited because Leanne had reserved a stable just for me!

It seemed to take forever for them to be completed, but finally the big day arrived for me to move in to my new home. Leanne had filled my stable with fresh sweet-smelling sawdust, I had a lovely new feed bucket hanging from the door, and I was even allowed to have a hay net jam-packed with tasty lucerne. Best of all, the back doors of each stable opened out into a sunny little yard for us to stand in and enjoy the view out to the day paddocks. As Leanne led me down the breezeway towards my stable at the end of the block, I started to feel a little bit nervous. It was rather a strange place; there were rakes and brooms leaning against walls everywhere, strange horses stared at me with wide eyes from the other stables, there were unfamiliar smells and the sound of my hooves echoed loudly on the concrete as I walked. I jumped to one side with fright as one of the doors opened near me unexpectedly and I snorted and danced about on the end of my lead. Leanne turned to look at me with smiling eyes and assured me that everything was fine and I just had to get used to it. She opened the door and I stood there peering fearfully into my new stable.

I thought I would love being an indoor horse but suddenly all I wanted to do was turn and canter back to my paddock as fast as my trembling legs would carry me! I arched my neck and sniffed the air in the doorway, wondering what terrifying horse-eating gremlins might be hiding in the corners waiting to pounce on me. But when I turned to look at Leanne and saw the amused expression on her face, I realised that I was being a little bit silly. Feeling reassured by her presence, I stepped inside onto the sawdust. I looked around, I sniffed and snorted, I glanced back at the doorway and decided this was too much for me! I didn't like it at all! I quickly headed for the back door and stumbled out into the yard, longing for the fresh air and sunshine. Leanne was disappointed that I didn't like it and tried to coax me back inside but I wasn't having a bar of it! That night I slept outside, only going inside the foreboding gremlin-filled stable for a quick bite of hay or a sip of water. It would be about 2 weeks before I finally settled in and started to enjoy being pampered as a stabled horse. Looking back it seems hard to believe that I ever hated it!

Every morning Leanne would come to make my breakfast, take my rugs off and hang them up, brush me and then take me out to my day paddock. I loved going out for the day! Sometimes instead of walking, Leanne would run and I would canter along beside her as she held my lead rope loosely in her hand. When we got to my gate, she would laugh and wrap her arms around my neck as she told me she would see me later in the afternoon. As soon as she'd taken off my halter I would go flying off down the paddock, bucking and kicking and snorting with happiness and excitement. Then I would drop down and have a lovely big roll in the dust, scratching all the itches I couldn't get to overnight when my rugs were on. I felt like a spring filly again, it was heavenly! Leanne always stood watching my antics with a huge grin on her face and once I had settled down and started grazing she would hang my halter on the gate and go off to work for the day.

As much as I loved going out in the mornings, I was always ready and waiting at the fence for her to bring me in again in the evenings. When I saw her arrive I would whinny with delight and trot happily to the gate. Most nights she would climb up onto my back and ride me down to my stable while the sun was slowly setting below the hills around us. It really was a wonderful time in both of our lives.

Every so often I would get a different horse to share a day paddock with, and one day Leanne was told to put me out with a grey stockhorse named Jess. Jess never had paddock mates for very long because she was extremely aggressive and nasty, but Barry thought that because I was on older quieter horse she may not mind having me around. I wasn't too thrilled about the idea and knowing how unfriendly she was, I decided I would just keep my distance and stay away from her. She didn't really pay much attention to me anyway, unless I was at the water trough when she wanted a drink.

One afternoon a few days later, I was dozing by myself up at the top end of the paddock and Jess was about halfway down, standing under a tree. Leanne had arrived and was walking up the paddock holding a carrot and my halter, calling out to me to come down. I was half asleep and my hearing wasn't all that good anymore so I hadn't realised she was there. Jess was watching her and she must have spotted the carrot and decided she wanted it. She walked over to Leanne and started following her, sniffing and nudging at her trying to steal the treat out of her hand. Leanne pulled the carrot out of her reach and told her to shoo, and in that instant, mean old Jess got very angry.

I suddenly sensed that something was wrong and I opened my eyes and looked, just in time to see Jess spinning her back end around towards Leanne. Jess had her teeth bared and her ears pinned flat back

on her head and she squealed and swung a power-
ful double-barrelled kick at Leanne. Her pointy black
hooves narrowly missed hitting my poor friend
square in the chest as she quickly jumped back and
moved out of the way in the nick of time. You may
have heard the expression 'seeing red' when someone
is angry... well, I saw red. How dare that awful mare
try to kick my best friend! I was furious and without
giving it a second thought I leapt forward and came
thundering down the hill, snorting and tossing my
head angrily. I cantered straight down and came to a
sudden halt standing directly in between Leanne and
Jess, and although I knew she was very tough I looked
that nasty stockhorse right in the eye and dared her to
try to hurt my friend again.

I don't know whether it was my fury or the adren-
aline coursing through my veins but I was shaking
with rage, and I stomped my front hoof on the ground
and snorted as I flattened my ears against my head,
still staring down the unfriendly mare who suddenly
didn't seem so scary anymore.
I guess Jess must have realised I was extremely serious
because she backed off, tossed her head carelessly at
me and walked back to the tree she had been standing
under. I turned to Leanne to greet her and eat the carrot she had been holding and saw that she was looking
at me in complete amazement. She had goosebumps
prickling her skin and her eyes shone with tears. She
threw her arms around my neck and gave me a big
hug as she thanked me over and over again for com-

ing to save her. It had been a natural reaction for me but I could see that Leanne was very touched by my protective instinct towards her. That night I got extra molasses in my dinner, lots more lucerne hay than usual, and a lot of hugs!

The next day when Leanne arrived, she brought with her a piece of paper which she stuck on my stable door. It was a special poem she had written just for me and I would like to share it with you:

She gleamed silver in the sunlight
And moved silently through the grass like a ghost
A gentle spirit at one with her earth
The land she loved she had made her own
No fence would keep her in
No rope would hold her back
She was as free as a summer breeze at twilight
I watched her for hours that day
And knew nothing would ever be this close
to my heart again
She is the life that runs through my veins
Through her bright eyes I see a world
with no boundaries
And in her heartbeat I hear the sound of freedom
Pride and grace
Gentleness and an ancient wisdom unknown to man
She is an angel watching over me
Sharing my thoughts and creating my dreams

Running through the rivers of my soul
A wide-eyed child of the universe
She was there in the most difficult of times
And at night we looked at the stars
and dreamed together
She is my kindred spirit
My guardian angel
The only one I will ever let this far into my heart
No matter what secrets the future may hold
She will always be there with me
My dearest friend.

Chapter 11 – Stable memories

Now that I had settled in to my life as a posh stabled horse, things were going great. Leanne was still keeping a close eye on my diet and every few months she would collect a sample of my blood and take it to the vet for testing. My liver seemed to be fully functioning and I was feeling very lucky to be happy and healthy after so many other horses had perished. I was getting older though, and I wasn't completely without health issues.

In the summertime I had to be completely covered with a cotton rug, neck rug and a fly mask to protect my sensitive skin not only from the burning sun but also from the dry grass. I had developed an allergy to it in my later years and without my rugs the grass would make me itch like crazy. My hair would fall out in huge patches, I lost my appetite and my skin would swell up in big flat lumps. The vets never worked out why; they took tissue samples from me and tested me for autoimmune diseases but nothing ever showed up. I guess I was just particularly sensitive because of my Appaloosa colouring, especially around my pink-skinned eyes and muzzle.

One spot that was always driving me mad was the underneath of my belly. All year round, it was my absolute favourite place to be itched and Leanne would stand be

side me for ages rubbing my big tummy with a brush or scratching with her hands. Oh, it was bliss! I don't know why it was always so itchy but I just loved it. It felt so lovely that I would turn my head around and use the end of my nose to rub her on the arm or on her hand if she held it out for me. It was my way of grooming her back! Occasionally I would get a bit carried away and accidentally nip her with my big teeth so she was always a little bit wary of my offers for a return massage. Sometimes I would find a fallen branch in the paddock that was just at the right height for me to stand over and rub my belly on and I would end up with lots of little cuts and scratches all over me, but it was worth it!

One afternoon while Leanne was grooming me, she started to rub the brush under my belly and it was so nice that I lifted my back leg high into the air, leaning to the side with my eyes shut and my nose twitching wildly. I was lost in the moment; all I could think about was the heavenly brush scratching me. My leg rose higher and higher, I curled my hoof in and leaned even more to the side enjoying the blissful scratch... but unfortunately I leaned a little too far. All of a sudden I realised I was totally off-balance and it was too late to right myself. I started to tip further and further and then CRASH! I fell heavily onto my off-side, hitting the metal fence of my yard as I went. It didn't really hurt, it just shocked me and feeling very embarrassed I quickly jumped to my feet and shook the dust from my side. Leanne didn't know what to do, she was just as surprised as I was, but once she realised I was not injured she started to laugh. I looked over to see Monty, Kaz's big fleabitten grey gelding, snorting at me with amusement. He flicked his tail as if to say 'nice one, idiot' then turned and walked snootily into the shade of his stable. If horses could blush, my cheeks would have been bright red!

While I was living in my stable at LYH, Leanne moved into a small flat in Wanniassa, a few suburbs away, with her boyfriend who she'd been with for about 18 months. His name was Liam and I didn't like him at all. Sometimes when Leanne came to feed me she would tell me about nasty things he had said or done to upset her, and I could sense her distress. He was always seeing other girls behind her back, and he told her lie after lie to cover his tracks.

Not long after they moved in together, she came down with a terrible flu and became so sick and dizzy that she couldn't even get out of bed. She asked Liam if he would go up to LYH, take my rugs off and let me out of my stable on his way to work because she was too sick. He promised her that he would, and when she rang him later in the morning and asked if he'd done it he said yes. He strangely didn't get home from work until very late that day, around 8:30 at night, and Leanne was still very ill. She had been waiting for him to come home so that he could drive her up to feed me, and when she asked him to take her he got very angry and refused. She begged him until he finally agreed, although it was obvious he didn't want to.

When they arrived at the stables, Leanne slowly pulled open the heavy barn doors and walked into the breezeway. My stable was right up the end and as she walked towards it she realised that as usual, Liam had lied to her. He hadn't come up that morning to let me out at all, and I was very upset.

As soon as I saw her, I began whinnying frantically and pacing back and forward across the front of my stable. I had been locked in all day; the back doors that led out to my yard were closed because it was winter time, and I had been wearing my thick itchy doona rugs since the night before. My stable was filthy, the sawdust was full of manure because it hadn't been cleaned since the night before, and I was absolutely starving. I had finished my feed and eaten all of my hay overnight and because Liam was too lazy, I had never been given my breakfast or been let out to graze.

Leanne took one look at me in my dirty stable, starving, my eyes rolling back in my head with distress, and she burst into heartbroken tears. She was horrified that Liam had left me this way, but he didn't care at all. Despite the fact that she was so sick, he didn't offer to help clean my stable or mix my feed; he just went and sat in his ute sulking. After that, she never asked for his help with me again. It wasn't like he didn't know what he was doing; after all, he had owned several horses and used to go to shows and pony club. He was just lazy, uncaring and not to be trusted but she took a very long time to figure that out. I'll tell you more about him later...

Over the years I'd had so many accidents and ailments and unfortunately they continued to happen throughout my twilight years. One lovely sunny day, Leanne arrived to take me for a nice relaxing ride around the property. I was looking very trendy with my matching purple saddle cloth and boots and I felt great as we stepped out of the stables for our little adventure in the sunshine. We headed off down the road, past the round yard and the arena and down a dirt trail that went along the top of a large dam near the paddock I had previously shared with Moppy. It was a different dam to the one Jake and I used to splash around in, we had ridden past it many times but had never been very close to it so Leanne decided that we would wander down and ride around the edge of it. This seemed like a grand idea! It was quite warm so I thought I might even be able to have a splash in the cool shallows. We turned and made our way down a wallaby track winding around the side of the dam until we were right beside the water. It was rather nice, there was a mother duck with her ducklings going for a swim and a large gumtree nearby provided shade as we walked along. Little did I know what awaited us just a few steps ahead...

We had only made our way around a small section of the big dam when without warning the ground beneath my front feet gave way and I plunged violently down into thick squelchy mud. It had looked completely normal, like solid ground, but the water's edge was like quicksand. My front legs were stuck in the mud up to my knees and I snorted with fear and surprise as I struggled desperately to pull myself free. Leanne was frantically trying to get me to back up but the more I tried to get out, the deeper I sank. I couldn't keep my balance as my hooves disappeared further and further down into the mud and right at the moment when Leanne jumped out of the saddle, I crashed down onto my side, half buried in mud and half lying in the water. My back legs had now sunk down into the sticky awful mud too and I started to panic as I thrashed around, desperate to escape. Leanne stood on the solid part of the bank pulling on my reins for dear life, trying to help me get out but I sunk more and more until the mud and filthy water was up over my flank. She ripped off her boots, threw them on the grass and strode into the mud to try to save me.

She reached down into the muck until she found my girth and undid it, pulled the saddle from my back and tossed it onto the bank, trying to make it as easy as possible for me to get out. She was talking to me, trying to keep me calm and tell me that everything would be fine but I could sense her fear and hear the tremor in her voice. By now I was shaking all over with terror and I was becoming exhausted from trying to pull myself out of the mud. I was starting to give up; I was going to drown right there in that innocent-looking dam, and I laid back onto my side trembling and gasping for air.

Leanne moved around to crouch beside me in the horrible mud and she held my heavy head up out of the water for me so that I could rest. I was so grateful; every muscle ached and burned from the effort of trying to pull my big heavy body up out of the dam. As I lay there looking up past the high gumtree branches to the clouds moving majestically through the sky, I decided I was going to muster every ounce of strength I had left and give it one more go. I took a deep breath, filled my lungs with sweet fresh air, and using my powerful back legs I pushed up as hard as I could and lurched forward. Again and again I repeated this manoeuvre and I felt the suction of the mud breaking as my legs came free. Another big leap forward and I felt the firm soil of the bank beneath my front feet. I dragged myself forward, scrambling at the dirt with my hooves until finally I was out! Leanne cheered and yelled and pulled me away from the edge. I could barely stand, my knees were weak and I could feel the mud sliding down my belly and legs. I stood there puffing and panting until I stopped shaking, and Leanne led me slowly back up the hill to the stable block.

When we got there she took me straight to the wash bay, and as she hosed the stinking mud off me she told me her next move would have been calling the fire brigade to rescue me if I hadn't been able to free myself. Imagine that, little old me getting saved by the fire brigade! I wonder if it would have made the news... either way I'm glad I didn't have to find out. That night after a lovely big dinner, I dropped my aching body down into the soft sawdust in my stable and slept and slept.

Chapter 12 – Not the vet again!

For a few peaceful months since my muddy near-death experience beside the dam, life had been blissfully quiet and uneventful. I was enjoying living in my lovely stable, and going out to my paddock every morning to laze and graze away the days. Dear old Moppy was also living a lazy stress-free existence in a nice shady paddock at the front of LYH. Barry had moved him to that paddock because he thought it was so nice for people to see the lovely old clydesdale as they drove in through the front gate.

One night as I was munching away enjoying a delicious feed of lucerne chaff, pellets and molasses, Leanne was busily brushing my speckled coat and picking out my hooves to make sure no sticks or stones were stuck in them. When she had finished grooming me, she stood watching me as she leaned against the doorway of my stable in the dimming late evening light. She always seemed to love being at the stables at that time of day, as the sun slowly sank down below the outline of the mountains leaving the sky awash with streaks of blazing pink and orange. High above our heads, a mob of cockatoos screeched and squawked to each other as they searched for the perfect gnarled old gum tree to settle into for the night. Feeling relaxed and enjoying Leanne's company, I lifted my head from my bucket for a moment to look at her and give her an affectionate snort from my chaff-covered nostrils. As I stared at her she tipped her head to one side and looked at my nose, her eyebrows furrowing in concern. Assuming that I must have had a chunk of sticky sweet molasses stuck to my whiskers, I quickly rubbed my face and muzzle on my front leg but as I did so Leanne marched forward and grabbed my halter. She held my head still as she looked closely at my nostrils and I could tell from the firm grip she had on me that something was wrong. After a minute or so she let go of my halter and told me there was a strange lump on my nose and that she would keep an eye on it. I hadn't noticed anything, I felt just fine!

A couple of weeks later Leanne was hosing me down in the wash bay, as I greedily scoffed myself on the rich green pick that surrounded the concrete slab I was standing on. The grass was lovely there because it was always getting watered when people washed their horses! I chewed happily on a mouthful of sweet delicious clover and shut my eyes as I shook droplets of cool clear water from my ears. What a beautiful day it was! Just then I noticed Leanne had wandered over to Kaz and they were talking with their arms crossed as they both stared at me. Curious, I pointed my ears as far forward as they would go and strained to hear what they were saying. On the breeze I caught snippets of 'it's definitely much bigger than it was' and 'might need to get the vet out'. They must have been talking about that pesky lump on my muzzle. Yes, it most certainly had gotten bigger because now when I grazed I could feel it, as if a big round pebble was inside my nose. It was getting quite annoying to be honest.

The next afternoon, Leanne had a vet out to inspect the irritating mysterious lump. He poked, prodded and squeezed it until it hurt and I jerked my head back out of his reach and swished my tail angrily. Grumpy and feeling well and truly bothered by his presence, I pinned my ears back and thought about biting him right on his skinny bottom as he bent over and searched through the dusty plastic box of equipment he'd brought with him. Just as I was baring my teeth and feeling particularly wicked, he straightened up and turned to face me. My wickedness quickly turned to sheepish guilt as he smiled and offered me one of my favourite snacks- a big piece of Luv-a-Lic horse liquorice! I gratefully accepted the delicious treat and, still feeling guilty, I sniffed at him warmly as he clapped me on the neck and scratched behind my ear. He told Leanne that at this stage he wanted to leave the lump alone because I was quite an old horse and the trauma of surgery could put too much pressure on my body, especially considering the problems I'd had with my liver from the Paterson's curse. He instructed Leanne to ring him again if the lump got much bigger, and then he left.

Unfortunately it was only a few weeks before she had to call him again, because the lump had become the size of a golf ball and stuck out painfully from my muzzle, right inside the opening of my off-side nostril. The vet that arrived this time was my usual lady vet, who had seen me many times before. Rather than put me through the stress of trucking me to the vet for an operation, they decided to sedate me and remove the lump with just a local anaesthetic. She gave me a needle and after a couple of minutes I felt as if a heavy fog was surrounding me. I was very relaxed and sleepy and I swayed gently on my feet as I struggled to hold my head up. I felt stinging in my nose as local anaesthetic was injected around the lump but I was too tired to care. I couldn't really remember much of what happened after that but when the sedation finally wore off, the lump in my muzzle was gone and in its place was a line of stitches. It was very sore and I didn't eat very much for the next couple of days.

Leanne told me that the lump was something called a Granuloma and the vet suspected it may have been the result of a reaction to a bee sting or insect bite. When they had cut into my muzzle to remove it, the lump had a thick rubbery shell and inside that it was full of very hard crumbly granulated tissue (hence the name Granuloma I guess!). It looked a little bit like very coarse dark pink sand. Whatever it was, I was just glad it was gone! It took a couple of weeks for my poor nose to heal and once all the stitches were gone I was left with a deep scar in the soft skin of my muzzle. The relief I felt at being free of the granuloma didn't last long, however, as within a month it became obvious that the cursed thing was growing back again.

The vet had told Leanne that they had to make sure they removed every last bit of it, otherwise it would most certainly come back quite quickly. I guess that a tiny piece of it had escaped the vet's keen eye and now I would have to have more blasted surgery on the stupid thing! Leanne decided to leave it for a little bit longer before she put me through the second operation, and to make things worse the vet had recommended that I have it done over at their clinic this time.

A few weeks later with the lump steadily growing bigger in my nose again I was on my way out to the large animals vet hospital, in a float owned by one of Leanne's friends. When I arrived I was feeling very nervous and I was foaming with sweat. Leanne unloaded me from the float and led me to the stables. As I walked through the breezeway the familiar smell of sawdust and disinfectant hit my nostrils, and the hairs stood up along my withers. It reminded me of being in this place before, when I had surgery to remove the skin cancer from my eyelid.

I was only kept waiting for about an hour before a friendly young vet nurse came to get me and she took me to the sedation and recovery room. It was a small room with a rubber floor and padded walls where horses were sedated in preparation for surgery, and also where they were left to wake up if they have had a general anaesthetic. Just like when I had the lump removed the first time, the vet gave me a needle and I became very sleepy. When I came to, the lump was gone and once again I had a neat line of stitches in my muzzle. I was feeling very groggy and hot and as I stood in the soft sawdust resting, I heard Leanne's voice. A moment later her face appeared over the stable door and although I was pleased to see her I could barely even point my ears forward to say hello. She gave me a pat and a hug and looked sadly at my stitched-up nose, from which drops of blood would fall every minute or so. Leanne asked one of the vets why it was still bleeding and they said it was possible that because my liver had been so badly damaged during the Paterson's curse epidemic, my blood wasn't clotting as quickly as it should. They didn't know for sure though, and it did stop later that afternoon.

While I recovered from my sedation, Leanne offered to help the busy nurses get an x-ray of a foal with an injured leg in the stable next to mine. Her job was to hold the foal's mother, a big chestnut mare who looked very cranky and unpleasant. While the nurses tried to keep the little foal still long enough to get the x-ray with a portable machine, Leanne held the lead rope of the mum and patted her on the neck in an attempt to distract her from what was happening with her baby. I was right when I said the mare looked cranky because all of a sudden she pinned her ears back, snaked her head around and bit Leanne- very hard, and right on the bum cheek!

It was both hilarious and horrifying at the same time, as the mare's big grass-stained teeth sunk into her flesh and bit down. Leanne shouted in surprise and spun around to face the nasty mare, the shock and pain clearly showing on her face. The nurses couldn't help but laugh and Leanne did too, it was very funny, but she was in so much pain that she had to lie down on the cold concrete floor of the breezeway and wait for her poor throbbing backside to stop hurting. A little while later she went into the toilet and looked in the mirror to discover she had an enormous, shocking black and purple bruise where the mare had bitten her. She could hardly sit down for days and after that she couldn't even get back in the saddle for a couple of weeks. I was the one who'd had surgery but we both ended up needing healing time from that day!

I'm pleased to report that they successfully removed all of the granuloma the second time around so I was never bothered by it again. Leanne's bum cheek also made a full recovery, and she learned never to turn her back on an unfamiliar horse ever again!

Chapter 13 - Hoskinstown

In 2005, a few months after the unforgettable bum-biting incident (hee hee!), my nose was all healed up and I was feeling great. Leanne was not doing so well though. It seemed like she was sad all the time, and sometimes when she was brushing me and putting my rugs on at night I would catch her wiping silent tears from her tired-looking eyes. I knew exactly what my poor friend was sad about – that nasty smelly old boyfriend of hers, Liam. Just the thought of him made me wrinkle my nose up with disapproval!

Ever since she had started seeing him her whole world had been turned upside down, again and again. He was still always meeting up with other girls and telling Leanne lies about where he'd been, but he wasn't actually very good at lying so she always ended up catching him out. Her sadness was always easy for me to sense. It radiated from within her and hovered in the air around her like a cold heavy fog, and it made me feel sad right inside my big heavy old heart. My friend deserved better than this.

One morning Leanne arrived at the stables with some big news – we were going to be leaving LYH. Oh no! I loved it there! I was very unhappy to hear this, and I sulked and swished my tail with annoyance as she told me her plans. Her and that miserable boyfriend of hers had rented a small house on 5 acres, outside Canberra in a tiny village called Hoskinstown, and Moppy and I would be going to live out there the following weekend. Leanne said that there was a shed out there which had 2 stables in it, so I would still be able to enjoy my luxury indoor lifestyle. I guess that made it sound slightly better, but I couldn't believe that she was moving us out there with that silly boyfriend who kept breaking her heart.

The weekend rolled around in no time and as we travelled to Hoskinstown in a borrowed float, I thought about some ways I might be able to get rid of Liam. Maybe I could stomp my hoof on his foot really really hard, and make him so mad that he would go away and never come back! Or perhaps I could do a poo on his car, or bite him every time he walked past until he decided to move out! It all sounded good in my head, but as the float bumped and bounced up the driveway of our new home I knew in my heart that there was nothing I could do to change things. We were there to stay.

The nice thing about moving to Hoskinstown was that now Leanne and I actually lived together, and she could walk out and see me any time she wanted. There was always carrots and apples and slices of bread on offer, which Moppy and I were always happy to accept. There was one thing that took me by surprise though; as the days at our new home turned into weeks and I got to know Leanne's daily routine, I realised something. Life had really changed for her... somewhere along the way, she had grown up.

When I first met Leanne, things were so carefree in her life. She was young, she had her mum and dad looking after her and getting her everything she needed, and her lifelong dream of getting her very own horse had just come true, with me! When she wasn't at school, she would spend every spare minute she had at the paddocks. We would go for long rides, she would give me baths with this bubbly glo-white shampoo that made me extra clean and smelled good enough to eat, and we had all those amazing fun-filled days I was telling you about earlier in the story. But things were different now. Leanne had a full-time job, a troubled relationship, she had rent and bills to pay, and she always seemed so stressed. There had already been so many nights at Hoskinstown when I had heard angry shouting coming from the little house she shared with Liam. All they ever seemed to do was fight, I really didn't understand why they bothered to stay together at all.

In the middle of my paddock there was a small dam for us to drink from, and almost every evening when she got home from work, Leanne would come outside and sit beside the water by herself. She sometimes put headphones on and listened to music and she would sing quietly to herself and stare sadly at the water as the sun was setting. It was very peaceful out there and I think she preferred the quiet stillness of the dam to the hurt and anger that always raged inside the house. Sometimes I would wander over for a cool drink and stand close by so she would know I was there if she needed me. She liked to put her arms around my neck and rest her head against me, and she always breathed in so deeply as if she was trying to recharge herself on my dusty, horsey scent. As much as I loved her cuddles, I really missed seeing her happy.

One night I was dozing in my stable in the shed next to the house, when I was woken suddenly by the sound of Leanne and Liam arguing again. It sounded different this time though, Leanne's voice was desperate and distraught and Liam sounded frighteningly angry. I put my head out over the stable door and strained my ears to listen, and I heard a big loud thud and then a lot of crashing and banging. Leanne was crying loudly and then all of a sudden the front door flew open and she came running frantically out of the house. It was a very cold late-autumn night and I can still clearly remember that she was wearing bright yellow flannelette pyjamas with pictures of smiling bumble bees all over them, and her feet were bare as she ran desperately out into the darkness.

As I stood there, locked in my stable and watching on in horror, Liam came racing out of the house behind her. His face was contorted with rage and he ran after Leanne as she tried to escape barefoot through the paddock into the cold dark night. When he caught up to her, he grabbed her from behind in a big angry bear hug, picked her up, and as she cried and kicked and screamed for him to let her go, he carried her back into the house and slammed the front door shut behind them. I could hear his boots stomping loudly on the timber floor, then the bedroom light was turned on. I heard him shout at her 'NOW STAY THERE' and there was the sound of another door being slammed closed. The little house fell silent then, and all I could hear was the sound of my own heartbeat thundering loudly in my ears.

I was so angry and upset at what I had just witnessed, but I was stuck in my stable and I couldn't even try to help her. I paced back and forth angrily, I snorted and tossed my head and stomped my feet, and I wondered whether I would be strong enough to kick the solid wooden stable door down. I didn't sleep a wink that night, the darkness seemed to last forever and as the sun slowly came up the next morning I waited anxiously for Leanne to come outside. Eventually I heard the sound of footsteps and then she appeared at my stable door. Her eyes were still red and glassy from crying and she looked very tired as she let Moppy and I out into the paddock. I rubbed my face gently on her arm and sniffed at her softly to let her know I was worried about her, and then I watched sadly as she got into her car and headed off to work. One day soon, in her own time, she would realise that life wasn't supposed to be like this.

Despite all the sadness there was one great thing that happened while we were living at Hoskinstown; we got 2 new friends to join our little family! The first one was a lovely little puppy which Leanne named Max. He had been born at Liam's parents farm in Michelago; his mum was a Labrador and his dad was a mixture of kelpie, collie and heeler. Max was chocolate brown and white with tan on his legs and face and he really was beautiful. He followed Leanne around everywhere and he would often hide in the grass and stalk her, with his belly dragging on the ground and his green and gold eyes glued to her in concentration. He would sneak along on his tummy, creeping closer and closer, and then he would wiggle his little bum and pounce up at her like a playful kitten, jumping all over her as she laughed and scratched him behind his ears. After a while he started getting called 'Max-a-Million the 2-dollar dog' and he was a happy funny little light in our lives. They say dogs are a good judge of character and I think that's pretty true because Max didn't like that nasty Liam at all and would never do anything he tried to tell him to do, like sit or stay or stop barking.

The other new friend that we got was a hilarious and naughty billy goat, who, funnily enough, was named Billy. Leanne bought him from a lady who lived in the village of Murrumbateman, for the princely sum of 20 dollars, and she often said that it was the best 20 bucks she ever spent! Billy was a real character, he was rebellious and rude and so naughty but he was so funny at the same time. While Leanne was at work during the day, he would get bored so he would wander over to the fence, jump over it ever so casually and go hang out with the next door neighbour's cattle for the day. In the evenings when Leanne would get home, he would hear her car, call out with a loud maaa and then come bounding across the paddock, pop back over the fence effortlessly and run over to greet her and see if she had anything for him to eat. He had strange yellow eyes and an impressively long beard sprouting from his chin and I found him to be a rather fascinating creature. He really took a liking to Moppy for some reason and they were quite an odd pair to see together: the huge gentle horse with his haystack mane and big fluff-covered feet, and the weird shaggy little bearded goat. Whenever it rained, Billy would go and stand under Moppy's belly and hide so he wouldn't get wet and it always made me giggle.

Billy really liked to eat, and I mean he would eat almost anything. My food, the dog food, Leanne's food, and especially the nice little plants that grew in the garden around the house. The house yard was fenced off and the gate was always shut to keep us out, but that didn't stop the silly little goat from getting in. He just bounced over the fence whenever he pleased, and Leanne would eventually notice him chewing away on her garden and run out to shoo him back into the paddock. She had one plant that was very special, so special that she kept it in a pot up on top of a fridge that sat on the front verandah. It was a tiny little baby pine tree, but not just any pine tree. Leanne and her mum had bought it in the village of Bungendore on Anzac Day earlier that year and it had been grown from seeds collected from the Lone Pine in Gallipoli, which was the scene of a terrible battle for Australian and Turkish soldiers during World War 1 way back in 1915. Leanne's great grandfather had been injured in that very battle so the tiny tree in the pot had great sentimental value to her.

One afternoon I was grazing near the dam and Billy came wandering over from the direction of the house to get a drink. As he got closer to me, I could see that he was chewing on something that looked very tough and difficult to eat. The crazy animal had probably pulled some washing off the line, it wouldn't have surprised me at all if it was a sock or something in his mouth. Billy was eyeballing me with that unpredictable wild stare of his, which honestly made me a little bit nervous, so I cautiously backed away from him and carried on grazing further down the paddock. I didn't think anything of it again... until Leanne got home later that day.

She came buzzing up the driveway in her little beige Subaru Brumby ute, parked and got out, and walked up onto the front verandah fumbling for the house key on her keyring. She was just about to unlock the door when she glanced to the side where the fridge was, looked away, froze suddenly, then looked back again at the fridge. Ohhh no. Beside the fridge on the weathered old timber boards of the verandah was a trail of spilled dirt. As Leanne lifted her gaze from the small pile of dirt to the top of the fridge, she gasped in horror and put her hand over her mouth. There, sitting on the top of the fridge where it should have been perfectly safe, was the pot that the little pine tree had been growing in... but the tiny tree was gone, and where it had stood there was nothing but an ominous hole in the soil.

As I realised, at the same time as Leanne, that the goat must have gotten to it, I looked around to see where he was. He was standing by the fence near the stables, with his creepy yellow eyes peacefully closed as he snoozed in the late afternoon sunlight. I looked back at Leanne and she too had spotted the offending tree-eater, and she was not happy. She threw her handbag and keys to the ground and came charging furiously out of the house paddock, with her sights set firmly on Billy. The sound of her angry footsteps rushing towards him made him wake suddenly and just as she had almost reached him, he sprung to life and went running madly away from her. She yelled at him and called him a few interesting names, which I better not repeat, and she chased after him but he was too quick and agile for her and he went skimming neatly over the fence into the neighbour's paddock. He bounced off into the middle of the herd of cows that lived there then turned and stood staring defiantly at Leanne, as if he was daring her to come get him.

She stood at the fence line and shouted at him that he was an idiot and if he thought he was going to be getting fed tonight he had another thing coming, then she turned and stormed back to the house. Moppy had been standing under a tree not far away, dozing, and the big lazy sod had slept right through the entire ridiculous display! I did feel very sorry for Leanne as I watched her sadly sweep up the dirt and carry the now-empty pot over to the shed. She had really loved that little pine tree, and she never did find another one that had been grown from that infamous Lone Pine. She also never figured out how the infuriating goat had managed to reach it up on the top of the fridge, but it wouldn't be the only time he did it.

Chapter 14 – Stormy skies ahead

As it turned out, we didn't end up staying at Hoskins-town all that long. The lady who owned the property decided she wanted to sell it, and since Leanne and Liam weren't in a position to buy it they started look-ing for somewhere else for us all to live. It wasn't long before they found a beautiful big house in a village called Burra, and once again we packed up and got on a float to move to our new home.

The property at Burra really was pretty. It was set on 10 acres of shady, crisp-smelling bushland and along with the house it had a lovely old timber shed, a chook pen, and a huge dam that was almost overflow-ing with cool sweet-tasting water. The whole place had a calm, tranquil feel about it and I liked it very much. The only problem was that grass doesn't grow very well in that bushy type of environment, so there wasn't much for Moppy and I to eat. The ground was hard and arid-looking around the gnarled old trunks of the eucalyptus trees that covered the property, and it wasn't long before I could feel my belly growling at the lack of decent feed for us to graze on. It didn't bother Billy at all though, if he got hungry he would just bounce over the fence into the house paddock and nibble on the rose bushes, or sample the various tasty-looking trees that grew around the yard. The rent at Burra was much more expensive than it had been at Hoskinstown, and now to top it off Leanne had to pay for a constant supply of hay to keep Moppy and I fed. It was a beautiful place but in the time that we lived there it was tough on all of us, for a few different reasons.

The peacefulness of the bush was regularly interrupted at night by the sound of Leanne and Liam's arguments. Leanne was always upset that there were so many nights when Liam just wouldn't come home, wouldn't tell her where he was or even answer his phone, sometimes for days at a time. Then when he would eventually turn up, he would still refuse to tell Leanne where he had been or who he had been with, and then they would fight some more. A few times I heard him talking on his phone out in the yard, flirting and laughing with some girl while Leanne was up in the house. I wished more than anything that there was some way I could tell her what was going on, but frustratingly I knew there was nothing I could do.

One night at Burra there was a huge, very frightening thunderstorm. The clouds had been gathering all afternoon, looking dark and foreboding as they rolled in over the horizon. I could smell rain and feel the charge of electricity tingling in the air, so Billy, Mop and I had settled in for the night in a gully down near the dam, where there was a thick pocket of trees to shelter us from any wind and rain that might come in with the storm. Liam hadn't come home for the previous 2 nights, and Leanne was up in the house with only faithful little Max-a-Million the 2-dollar dog to keep her company. He was the best kind of company when she was sad; he knew when her heart was breaking and he would lie beside her on the lounge with his head on her leg and gaze lovingly at her until she made eye contact with him. Then when she would look at him, he would wag his happy tail and push his warm wet nose into her hand for a pat, and he always made her smile and stopped her from feeling too lonely.

On this particular night, when the storm came, Leanne was standing at the kitchen sink washing the dishes and loyal Max was lying at her feet snoozing. The wind was howling, the trees were blowing furiously back and forth and deafening claps of thunder crashed through the sky one after another. I was huddled in the trees with my rump turned towards the wind, trying to get some sleep but the wild weather was making me nervous and I shifted my weight restlessly from one back foot to the other. I turned my head to look up at the house where my poor lonely friend was still standing at the kitchen window washing her dishes. All of a sudden a huge blue bolt of lightning appeared out of nowhere, snaking down from the clouds, and it connected directly with the power pole right in front of the house.

When it hit, there was an enormous flash and for a

split second the entire yard lit up like it was daylight. There was a terrifyingly loud BANG, a shower of sparks as something on the power pole exploded, and then there was only darkness. All of the lights inside the house went out, the dull distant sound of voices coming from the TV suddenly stopped, and everything was black.

Inside the house, Leanne was staring out of the window in horror with little Max cowering and shaking at her feet, both of them terrified by the huge bang of the lightning strike. The room was pitch black, she was all alone in the big empty house and she had no idea what to do.

I made my way to the gate at the top of the driveway and waited to see if she was ok, and after a few minutes the front door opened and Leanne cautiously wandered outside with a small torch in her hand. The driveway was littered with shattered pieces of the ceramic insulators from the power lines, which had exploded when the lightning hit. There was a strange burning smell in the air and I tossed my head nervously and snorted, trying to get the scent of it out of my nostrils. Suddenly I was startled by a noise coming from the trees behind me, and I spun around to see Moppy and Billy crashing out of the bushes wildly. Billy's weird yellow eyes were rolling around madly in his silly head and he stood at the fence for a second, stomped one front foot angrily as he sniffed the unpleasant electric smell in the air, then he did a ridiculous dramatic buck and went bouncing back into the safety of the trees. Moppy didn't really know what he was supposed to be doing, having been woken suddenly from his usual snoozing, so he yawned lazily and then turned and trotted awkwardly away, his enormous hairy feet crunching on sticks and dead leaves as he followed his odd little friend back into the bush.

I snorted and shook my head at them in disgust, then turned my attention back to the house and my poor friend who was all alone up there in the darkness. She was shining the dim little torch around looking at the debris all over the ground, and she could see that there was obviously serious damage to the power pole so she went back inside to call the electricity company for help. Just before she closed the door, I saw the glimmer of tears on her cheeks. My poor friend was already so stressed about her unfaithful, dishonest boyfriend and right now this was the last thing she needed.

Some workers from the electricity company arrived early the next morning, inspected the damage and told Leanne that unfortunately because it was a long weekend, it was going to take them a couple of days to get it repaired. This meant that she was in for some very long, lonely nights with no lights, no TV, not even any hot water. Later that day, since all the meat in her freezer was slowly thawing out, Leanne decided to use some of it to see if she could catch some yabbies in the dam. When she was younger she used to go yabbying with her friends all the time but now that she was older, and had to work and pay bills, she didn't have time for things like that.

She cut up some pieces of steak to use as bait and went to the shed where she found an old roll of fishing line, a small net and a bucket, then her and Max wandered down to the edge of the dam. I was curious to see what she was doing so I wandered over and watched as she tied one end of her fishing line to a stick, and on the other end of the line she tied a piece of meat. Then she placed the meat into the water, not too far from the edge, in the shallows where she could still see it. It wasn't long at all before a big blue yabby appeared out of the murkiness and started pulling at the meat. Leanne slowly dragged the line towards the water's edge, and then very quickly she pulled the meat upwards and scooped the surprised yabby into her net. Max wagged his tail and barked excitedly as she placed the yabby into the bucket, and then she dropped the meat back into the water.

She continued catching them for about an hour, one after another, and her bucket was getting quite full. She had just put a particularly big very dark-blue yabby into the bucket when she reached down to pick up the piece of meat again, but it was gone. She looked around, confused, searching for the meat which she knew she had only just placed on the ground right beside her. Where on earth had it gone? I could see that she was puzzled as she stood up and checked the ground where she'd been sitting again, and then she picked up the stick that the end of her fishing line was tied to and followed the line. To her surprise, the line was going up the bank of the dam... to where Max was lying, panting and smiling with his eyes fixed lovingly on Leanne. But Leanne's eyes were fixed on the fishing line, which, to her absolute horror, led directly into Max's mouth and down his throat. The silly mutt had eaten the piece of steak she'd been using for bait while she wasn't looking, without realising it had the string still attached to it!

'Oh no, Max!' Leanne cried, and she ran up the bank towards him. He was very pleased with himself, he'd enjoyed his tasty snack and he wagged his tail happily as Leanne crouched down beside him. She grabbed his muzzle and opened his mouth, to double-check that yes, he had most definitely swallowed her bait. Then she gently tried pulling the line out of his throat, which Max didn't like at all and he started to gag and make choking noises as he tried to get away from her. He pulled back and went to run, and as he did so, SNAP! The flimsy old fishing line broke and he took off into the paddock. Leanne looked very worried; if the fishing line got tangled up in his gut it could make him very sick or even kill him. She called the vet and spoke to them and they told her that if it was only a short piece of line it should pass without causing problems, but to keep an eye on him and bring him in if she was worried. Leanne watched him closely but nothing ended up happening, he was fine and didn't end up needing to go to the vet.

The day after that, Leanne was very relieved to see 2 trucks arrive to fix the damaged power lines. By the end of the day her electricity was back on and she was so grateful that she sent all of the repair men home with a dozen eggs each, freshly laid by her growing collection of colourful chickens that lived in the large chook pen in the house paddock. To my disgust, later that evening I heard the sound of a diesel engine pulling into the driveway and when I looked up from my hay to see who was here, it was Liam. He had been gone once again, for days, with no explanation. I had seen Leanne trying to call him over and over again, crying sometimes when he wouldn't answer because she knew he was with some other girl just like every other time before. He got out of his ute and Leanne came outside, crossed her arms defensively and stared at him. He asked what all the tyre tracks in the yard were from, and she told him about the lightning strike and how she had been alone with no power for the last couple of nights. To my absolute disbelief, that clown said to her 'why didn't you call me, I would have come home.' My blood boiled and I pinned my ears back fiercely thinking about how upset Leanne had been over him. Grrr, I wanted to gallop over there and bite him so badly! For the life of me I couldn't figure out what she saw in him, but once again she let him walk back into the house and back into our lives that day, and once again I waited for the next time he would inevitably shatter her heart into a thousand pieces. That silly, silly girl.

Chapter 15 – Burra to Michelago and beyond

Beside the front door of the house at Burra, there was a large timber box for storing firewood in. On the lid of it, someone who had lived there before us had stapled a comfy-looking dog mattress to it for their faithful friend to have somewhere to sleep. I never saw Max jump up there and use it, but that silly crazy goat was always getting into the house paddock and hopping up there for a sleep. Leanne would get home from work and there would be Billy, curled up neatly on top of the wood box looking very comfortable! He would greet her with a loud maaaa and then jump down and sniff at her curiously, hoping for a treat. His stomach was a bottomless pit when it came to eating, he just never stopped.

Not long after we moved to Burra, Leanne's nana gave her a beautiful Cyclamen plant as a housewarming gift. It was so pretty, the leaves were laced in a delicate detailed pattern and it was covered in glorious flowers. It needed to be kept in a cool shady spot, so Leanne placed it carefully up on top of the fridge on the front porch. I remember thinking to myself hmmm, this looks familiar, that was where she kept the pine tree when we lived at Hoskinstown! There was nothing on either side of the fridge for the goat to jump on, so I guess Leanne figured Billy wouldn't be able to reach it. Boy was she wrong. The lovely little plant didn't even make it through the first day before the hungry goat sniffed it out. Leanne came home from work to find the ceramic pot it had been in smashed all over the pavers, dirt everywhere, and no sign of the cyclamen. The mystery of the far-reaching plant-eating goat continued; none of us had any idea how he managed to reach it, and the silly wild creature never gave up his secrets. He just snorted dramatically and stomped his feet when Leanne told him off, and she never had the heart to tell her nana what had happened to the beautiful housewarming gift.

One day Leanne noticed that Billy had several dags that had formed in his cashmere hair; the dags were like matted dreadlocks and they were hanging from his belly and flanks. While he was resting on the wood box, she went out with a pair of scissors to try to cut them off and tidy him up a bit. Billy was calmly lying there watching her and when she started snipping at his belly hair his eyes opened as wide as they could go and he snorted in protest, but surprisingly he didn't try to get up and run away.; he was so arrogant that I guess he liked the attention. Things seemed to be going well as Leanne carefully cut away the dags, but then all of a sudden disaster struck!

Even though she was trying so hard to be careful, she accidentally snipped Billy's skin with the large blades of the scissors. It didn't actually cut him, it just pinched him, but he was very upset about it. He let out a sudden and very noisy unhappy-sounding MAAA and then leapt up and stomped one front foot furiously at Leanne, snorting and shaking his head, his crazy eyes almost burning right through her he was so angry. Then he leapt down off the wood box, went bounding madly through the yard, over the fence and he disappeared into the paddock. We could still hear him maaing and grunting as he crashed around wildly in the gumtrees. All that time while he was making a scene and having his tantrum, poor Leanne was standing at the front of the house, still holding the scissors and looking very shocked at Billy's sudden outburst. The wild-tempered goat was so angry with her for almost cutting him that he wouldn't let her go anywhere near him for 4 days, but during that time he still jumped into the house paddock when she wasn't home, to nibble the roses and check out what scraps the chooks were eating.

One warm sunny day I was delighted when Leanne came down to catch me and she told me we were going out for a ride. She was so busy and distracted with her life these days that she barely ever found time to take me out anymore. Things had changed so much for us and I still really missed our younger care-free days together. She brushed my smooth spotted coat, picked out my feet, and saddled me up. As we headed out the front gate I could smell the tangy eucalyptus trees and the warm festive scent of pine needles, and I breathed it all in deeply while we walked along the dusty dirt road. Leanne had told me we were riding up to visit a friend of hers who also lived in Burra, and he bred quarterhorses. I was excited to see them, as I myself was part quarterhorse! The sun was beaming down on us as we made our way along the winding uphill road and a dark sheen of sweat broke out on my shoulders, but I didn't care. It was a perfect day, out in the sunshine with my best friend, just like old times. She reached down and patted me on the neck as she sung along to a Dixie Chicks song she was listening to on her mp3 player. While she was in the saddle, her mind was clear and she forgot about her stresses and worries for a while.

It took about 45 minutes to ride to her friend's house, and I was very impressed when we got there. It was a horsey haven! The long driveway was lined with neat white timber fencing, there were fat shining horses grazing on rich green grass in the paddocks, there was a huge stable block, a round yard and a big sand arena. It was much more glamorous than the bushy scrubby paddock that I lived in and my mouth watered as I gazed at the delicious sweet-looking grass that grew there. Leanne's friend came out to greet us and I liked him at once. He was very friendly and kind and he patted me warmly and told Leanne that he liked me very much. He showed Leanne where she could tie me up, and they left me to happily stuff my face with lush grass while they went for a walk around the property. They spent a lot of time standing in front of a paddock at the top of the driveway near the front gate, and I could see them talking as Leanne patted a stunning big chestnut horse at the fence. He was strikingly handsome, his bright coat shone like silk in the sun and he had 4 white socks and a big white blaze that ran all the way down his face. I wondered what they were talking about for so long, but I was too busy eating to worry about it and after we headed home that day I didn't give the beautiful chestnut horse another thought. I didn't realise at the time, but we would meet him again later on.

When we had been living at Burra for almost 6 months, Leanne and Liam decided they didn't want to renew their lease on the house. It was very expensive, not at all suited to horses and much like Hoskinstown it had only been a place of bad memories for Leanne and their relationship. It was decided that they would move into a small cottage on Liam's parents farm at Michelago, where they wouldn't have to pay so much rent and there was proper feed in the paddocks for Moppy and I. I didn't even feel sad to leave Burra; it had looked so lovely at first, but it really hadn't turned out to be a nice place for any of us. There was one very sad thing about leaving though.

Down the road at Michelago, Liam's parents had a beautiful garden which they had been working on and landscaping for years. There were stunning ornamental trees, lots of bright colourful flowers, neat rows of hedges and pretty sandstone retaining walls surrounding pristine green manicured lawns. It was lovely... but it was also strictly a goat-free zone. Liam's parents had made it very clear that under no circumstance was Billy allowed to come to Michelago with us. As strange and eccentric as he was, I really liked him and I was very sad to have to say goodbye to him. About a week before we packed up and moved out, Leanne arranged for a friend from work who lived down the road to come and pick him up. Moppy was the saddest of all, he loved his shaggy little goat friend, and when the ute came buzzing up the driveway to take Billy away Moppy had to rub his face on his big furry front leg to wipe away his tears. Leanne had been feeling ok about Billy leaving, because she knew he was going to a good home where he would be well cared for and that was the most important thing. I don't think the realisation of him going really hit her until he was actually leaving though.

She greeted the man in the ute when he arrived at the top gate, and together they walked over to where she had tied Billy up. He always wore a bright blue collar around his neck so that if he escaped people would know someone owned him and he was a pet. She untied the rope and led him to the back of the ute, which had a stock crate on it ready to take the little goat to his new home. Billy sniffed at the cage and rolled his eyes wildly, in the same crazy way he always did when he was angry or unsure of something. The man lifted him up and put him into the crate, and quickly closed the gate behind him so he couldn't get out. Moppy's big rubbery bottom lip was quivering and I could see his dear old heart was breaking watching his little mate being taken away. It was all so sad and I nuzzled him on the shoulder affectionately to try to comfort him as he sighed, pinned his ears back sadly and dropped his lovely big head slowly to the ground, a crestfallen horse.

Billy was very angry at being put into the cage on the ute and he glared fiercely at Leanne and stomped his little front foot defiantly, snorting loudly out of his nostrils and tossing his head as he demanded to be let out. Leanne told the man to let her know how he settled in at his new home, and then the ute started up and off they went, carrying our fierce-hearted little friend away, out of our lives forever. Leanne had tears shining in her eyes as she called out a sad goodbye to him, and as the ute pulled out of the front gate and headed off down the road Billy must have realised he was leaving his home and he started to maa loudly, over and over again. He sounded so upset and distressed, and Leanne burst into tears and put her hands over her face as we heard him crying out desperately all the way down the road. It was awful, the poor little goat. I stood at the fence and arched my neck out towards Leanne, and she came over and wrapped her arms around me. She was so upset, and I gently rested my head over her shoulder and closed my eyes, sad about what had just happened but enjoying the cuddle. I really couldn't wait to leave this place, it seemed like it had been nothing but heartache for us all since the day we got here.

The following weekend we moved down the road to Michelago. It was so pretty there, we were finally out of the bush and into a lovely big paddock with a creek flowing through it and lots of beautiful big poplar trees dotting the fence lines. It seemed to be something of a trademark for the Monaro region, those pretty big poplar trees. Moppy and I roamed around, exploring our new home and enjoying the fresh juicy grass we had been missing so much since we'd moved to Burra.

A few weeks after we moved, Leanne came to feed me one evening and she said she had some sad but exciting news. She was going to be getting a new horse! Oh no, not this again. She chatted excitedly as she brushed my silvery coat and traced her fingertip over the large dark spots on my rump, telling me that her friend in Burra was giving her a horse that he'd had sitting in the paddock for years. It was the handsome shining chestnut with the white blaze that I had been admiring the day we rode there for a visit!

Well that certainly was exciting, but I wasn't sure what the sad part of the news was, so I lifted my head from my bucket of feed and looked at her quizzically. She stopped brushing me, sighed, and then said that the thing was, she was only allowed to have 2 horses at Michelago so Moppy was going to be leaving. Oh no! I swished my tail unhappily and tossed my head at her, wondering what on earth she was thinking. She said that because Moppy was so big, he ate a lot more than a normal horse and she was having trouble affording enough feed for him. It also cost her double the standard rate to get his feet trimmed by the farrier, and generally everything he needed was bigger and more expensive, so she had decided that she would lease him out for a while and see how the new horse went. She had arranged for a family that lived in the Tinderry mountains behind Michelago to take him; they already owned a few horses and they sounded very nice. A few short days later, Moppy was loaded onto a float and taken to his new home. I was so sad to see him go that I felt sick. This didn't seem right, he was part of our family! I could only hope that he would be happy and loved with his new people; unfortunately, it would turn out to be the opposite, but I'll tell you about that a little bit later.

After Moppy had gone, the new horse was picked up and brought to Michelago. As he stepped off the float he pranced on the spot proudly, flared his nostrils and arched his strong muscular neck and I remember thinking he must be the most beautiful horse I had ever seen. Leanne led him over to the paddock and let him go and he took off, galloping and pig-rooting through the grass as he whinnied and bucked with excitement. He spotted me standing at the fence watching, and he came cantering over to say hello. My heart thumped nervously in my chest and I wished like mad that Leanne had given me a bath and cleaned me up a bit before he got here. He was so handsome! He skidded to a halt in front of me and tried to greet me with a friendly curious sniff, but I felt so nervous and awkward that I squealed at him wildly and took a step backwards, unsure of what to do. He snorted in surprise and darted off into the paddock again, and I was immediately sorry for being rude to him.

I went cantering after him, feeling like a bumbling old nag compared to this sleek athletic-looking creature. After a minute he stopped running around and stood in the shade for a rest, so I joined him and introduced myself. He said his name was Frosty Jack, and he had been starting out his western show career until he had a terrible accident when he was 3 years old. He got his back leg very badly stuck in a fence and tore it open down to the bone, and also severed a major tendon. He wasn't really even lame from it but sometimes his foot would roll forward as he trotted and he would stumble. It had taken a very long time to heal because he had learnt to chew his bandages off, and they'd had to put a special wooden neck brace on him to stop him reaching around to pull his dressings off. He had a very large lumpy scar down his leg from the accident and his owners regretfully decided he was no good for the show ring anymore, so he had been turned out in the paddock and there he had stayed for 9 whole years. I couldn't believe it, this stunning looking horse had spent such a long time just doing nothing! I missed Moppy terribly, but Frosty was a lovely new friend to have and I was glad that he had come to live with me.

On the weekend of Australia Day, Leanne and Liam had another terrible fight. He had told her he was going with 'a friend' to the rodeo at Taralga, and when Leanne asked if she could come too, he said no and got very angry with her. Then Leanne had seen a text message on his phone about a girl he was planning on meeting at the rodeo, and she had gotten very upset and angry with him. She told me about it when she brought down my dinner the evening before Australia Day, and I shook my head sadly as I thought to myself 'well, here we go again.' Sure enough, early the next morning Liam got in his ute dressed in his cowboy clothes and drove away, leaving Leanne standing in the cloud of dust he left behind, heartbroken in the driveway. She stood there for several minutes, wiping away tears and kicking aimlessly at the stones on the ground as she contemplated what to do. Then suddenly she walked quickly back to the little cottage they were living in, grabbed a few things and went over to her ute. She called out to Max, and the happy green-eyed dog came running and leapt joyfully onto the back of the ute, where she clipped his chain onto his collar and gave him a loving pat on the head. Then she got into the driver's seat, started the engine and headed out the gate.

It was almost dark by the time she got home. Max looked very tired as he jumped off the ute and went to lie down on the cottage verandah. Leanne mixed up some feeds for Frosty and I and brought them down to the paddock gate and I sniffed at her, wondering where she had been. She smelled strange, like salt and summertime. She climbed up and sat on the gate and watched us eating, and she told us that she had decided she needed to get away for the day so she had taken Max for a drive to the beach.

Max loved to swim, and he had never been to the beach before so she had driven all the way to the coastal town of Bateman's Bay so he could swim in the ocean.

Along the way, Leanne and Max stopped in the pretty little town of Braidwood. They pulled up in front of a nice playground on the main road, and she let Max off the ute so he could go for a wee and have a cool drink. Then they headed off again until they got all the way through Bateman's Bay and out to a beach at a place called Broulee. Leanne had specifically chosen this beach because she had been there before and knew you were allowed to take dogs there. It had taken her just over 3 hours to drive to Broulee, and when Leanne led Max-a-Million the 2-dollar dog down through the sand to the water's edge, he was very excited! His little doggy eyes lit up and when she unclipped his lead he went bounding playfully into the ocean, where for about 20 seconds he ran and jumped and had a fantastic time. Then, he suddenly splashed some of the salty water into his eyes... and the fun was over.

Salt water stings quite a lot when you get it in your eyes, and Max discovered this the hard way. As his poor bright eyes started to sting, he yelped in surprise and then took off, running madly up the beach to escape the evil water that had so viciously attacked him. Leanne ran after him, calling out to him desperately and hoping he would stop before he got out to the busy road. He made it to the top of the sand, where the pathway to the carpark started, and he stopped and laid down on his belly. Leanne stopped running and called for him to come to her, but he refused to move. There was no way he was setting one paw on that beach again!

She called and called and Max just laid there panting and staring at her. She went to pick up his lead, clipped it to his collar and tried to make him come back to the water again, but he planted his feet firmly and flat-out refused to budge. Eventually she had no choice but to give up; he was done with the salt water and he would not be going anywhere near it again. They went back to the ute and drove down the street to the local takeaway shop, where she bought them some hot chips to share. They sat together on the tailgate of the ute, eating the tasty chips and throwing a few to the sea gulls, and then they headed off for the long drive back home. To this day when she is passing through Braidwood and the park where they stopped, Leanne still thinks of Max and their impromptu (and rather unsuccessful) road trip to the beach.

Chapter 16 – Friends
who became memories

In a fairly short space of time, we had moved house 3 times and said goodbye to 2 friends; Billy and Moppy. I'm very sorry to say that neither of those friends ended up with a happy outcome once they went away.

Little Billy, our shaggy yellow-eyed goat friend, was happy for a while. He went to his new home and he did settle in very well at first. Because he was so good at jumping fences, they decided to keep him tied up to start with so that he could get used to his new surroundings without running away and getting lost. He was tethered in their house paddock and grew fat and round eating lots of food scraps and hay, and his new owners liked him very much! Unfortunately, once they stopped tying him up, he did start jumping the fence and wandering off. He usually didn't go too far and would come back after a while, but one day when they went out to feed him, Billy was gone.

They waited and waited, and went looking for him

and called out to him, but no one knew where he had gone and he never ever did come home. I cried myself to sleep the night Leanne told me he had gone missing, thinking about him being lost in a strange place, wandering the hills looking for his old friends that he had loved. I hoped he didn't think that we hadn't loved him back, I couldn't bear the thought of it and it made my heart ache that I couldn't tell him we wished he hadn't had to leave. No one knows where he ended up, they never found him and we can only hope that he jumped a good fence and found a new family to love him, and that he was so happy with them that he never left again.

About a year after Moppy had been given to a family in the Tinderry mountains on a free-lease agreement, Leanne decided the time had come to offer him up for sale. She was very happy with Frosty, and she couldn't afford to take Moppy back again, so she contacted the people who had him and asked if they would like to buy him and keep him permanently. They behaved quite strangely and said that no, he was very expensive to feed and they couldn't afford to keep him so she should probably either sell him to someone else or come and get him. Leanne wondered why they hadn't just called her if they had wanted him gone, and she placed a 'for sale' ad in the newspaper classifieds that weekend to try to find him a new owner.

A family with a young teenage daughter contacted Leanne after seeing the ad, and asked if they could come and see Moppy. Leanne gave them directions on how to get to where he was, out behind Michelago, and they agreed on a day and time to meet out there. When that day came, Leanne drove out to the property and the people who had been leasing him went to get him from their paddock. As they appeared over the hill leading him, Leanne's heart skipped a beat and her stomach dropped. Moppy was almost unrecognisable.

He was skeletal. He was so horrifyingly skinny that every bone in his body was sticking out. Every rib was visible, his big square hip bones protruded from his emaciated frame and his huge gentle head appeared far too big for his body because he was so thin. He walked very slowly, as if every step was a massive effort because he was so weak. His hooves were very long and didn't look like they had been trimmed for the entire time that he'd been there, and his beautiful long haystack mane was tangled in enormous matted dreadlocks. The people who were coming to look at Moppy had arrived, and they were almost as shocked as Leanne to see the disgusting condition of the once-majestic big clydesdale.

Leanne struggled to find words as she apologised to the people for coming all this way only to find him in such a terrible state. She should have been checking on him to make sure he was being cared for. The family that had let him wither into this disgraceful neglected condition had nothing to say; they handed the lead rope to Leanne and repeated that he was too expensive to feed, and they went back into their house and closed the door. There was no apology offered, no explanation as to why they had let him get like this rather than just tell Leanne to come and get him months earlier. It was sickening.

Fortunately, the family who had come to see him were very compassionate and offered to take Moppy for a month as a trial, to see if they could fix him up. Leanne was very grateful and more than happy to agree to this, so the kind-hearted people arranged transport to bring him into Canberra. They got him a spot at an excellent agistment centre near the village of Tharwa and he even got his very own stable. They started feeding him up to get some weight back on him, they had his feet trimmed and they had a vet out to look at him too. The vet did some testing and found that he was severely anaemic due to malnutrition and was also riddled with parasites from not being drenched regularly. They also filed his teeth, and when Leanne came to visit and check on him after the first 2 weeks, he was already looking so much better. His new family quickly fell in love with the dear gentle old horse, and Leanne sold him to them cheaply, pleased to know he would now have the happy life he deserved.

About 5 years later, Leanne heard through a friend who had horses at the same Tharwa agistment centre that Moppy had sadly passed away. He had been about

25 years old, and he had started to suffer from liver failure. His devastated owners had been forced to make the difficult decision to end his suffering, and he had been put to sleep peacefully surrounded by the people who loved him. He was a lovely soul, a truly gentle soft-hearted giant and he certainly left an enormous hoof-print on my heart which will never fade away.

Vale Dakota Sam, our Moppy.

There's a saying that bad things tend to happen in threes, and for us that certainly rang true. Since we'd moved to Michelago Billy had disappeared from his new home, never to return, Moppy had been terribly mistreated and almost left for dead, and then there was the dreaded number 3… our beloved Max-a-Million.

During the months we spent living at Michelago Max had started to wander during the day, when Leanne was at work and he was left at home alone and bored. Sometimes he would be missing when she got home, and there were times when he didn't come back until the next day, or even a couple of days later. There had been reports of dogs killing sheep in the area, so Leanne had no choice but to start putting Max on a chain when she wasn't home. It wasn't much fun for him, but she knew that once dogs started killing sheep they would never stop, and farmers shot first and asked questions later.

For a few weeks, Max spent his days on the chain, miserable and unhappy. He would whimper and cry and chew things and dig holes out of frustration, but it was better than risking him being seen on someone's property where he shouldn't be if he wandered off again. One evening Leanne got home and went to let him off his chain, but he wasn't there. The chain was lying there in the dirt, and Max was gone. She started to look around, calling him and feeling very worried, when suddenly Liam's little brother Chris appeared and told her that he had let Max off for a run since he was home for the afternoon. He had meant well, he knew the poor dog was miserable being tied up and he had tried to do him a favour by letting him enjoy a few hours of free time. Leanne walked all the way around the property, calling out over and over, looking for her faithful two-dollar dog, but he didn't come back. All evening she searched for him, even driving up and down the road calling him from the car window, desperately hoping to see his brown and white face appear from the long grass. He was nowhere to be seen, and the next morning he was still missing. It was a Saturday, and that afternoon Leanne was using the computer in Liam's parent's office when Liam's dad appeared in the doorway. He looked at Leanne coldly, which was unlike him, and to her horror he said to her 'Your dog's dead. It was chasing sheep and they've shot it.' Then he turned and walked out, leaving Leanne broken hearted, shocked and crying in the hot dusty little office.

It was a difficult and strange feeling to lose a much-loved pet in such a way. He had disappeared, and apparently he was dead, but there had been no chance to say goodbye and no actual evidence of his demise to bring Leanne any closure. For several days she was in denial and part of her still held hope that Max would come home... but he never did. Eventually she approached Liam's dad and asked him where Max had been shot and what they had done with him, because she would like to go and collect him so she could bury him and say goodbye. He had been a loyal, comforting friend to her through some very difficult times in her life for the past couple of years and she wanted to put him to rest properly. Liam's dad was much more sympathetic to her that day than he had been previously in the office. He told her that he'd received a phone call from another property-owner who told him Max had been caught chasing sheep into a dam, along with his mother, the black Labrador named Lucy. They were running the frightened sheep into the water and then mauling their faces; both dogs had been shot and killed, and there was not an option to go and get either of their bodies unless Leanne wanted to face the furious grazier and pay for the stock that had been killed. It was a tough pill to swallow imagining beautiful loving Max doing that to those poor sheep, and Leanne had no choice but to accept his unpleasant fate and try to move on. Things started to fall apart in her life shortly after that, and at that time she didn't get a chance to properly grieve for her lost friend. A couple of years later, Leanne sat down and wrote the following poem for her Max when she was finally processing the tumultuous events of her life during those times:

Dear friend, it has been two long years
And I wonder, where are you now?
Time keeps passing me by
but still I think of you every day,
The sadness heavy in my heart like a cold grey stone.
Remembering you makes me smile,
fondly but bittersweet
The last time your faithful eyes stared into mine
The last time your smile greeted me at the gate
I wish I knew, I wish I could have known
That it was the last time we two friends would meet.
Thank you for your kindness and love so unconditional
I keep my memories of you buried deep in my heart
Where sometimes they come to life
and I feel you walking beside me
I am filled with regret to think that our time together was cut short
Gone in a fleeting moment, so brutal with the sting of farmer's lead
I will remember the good times, the best of times
When it was you and me against the world
And still I will miss you every day.
So be warm and safe high up in the stars, lost friend
And some day we will run laughing together
Through the green green fields of the sky.

Vale Max-a-Million, forever loved.

Chapter 17 – No more floats please

Things finally came to an end for Leanne and Liam the night before her 22nd birthday. She had caught him out again, cheating as usual, and at long last it was finally the straw that broke the camel's back. She'd had enough of his lies and his excuses, and I am proud to say that she started packing her things and left that very night. The worst relationship of her life was over and she was never going back.

That weekend she drove out to Michelago and loaded up the back of her little blue Jumbuck ute with the few belongings that she had, and Liam's younger brother Chris kindly offered to float Frosty and I into Canberra for her. I was absolutely thrilled when I found out she had arranged agistment for us at LYH, my old stomping ground! Leanne had moved back into her parent's house and I couldn't wait for us to get our life together back on track.

It was Sunday morning when Leanne arrived back at

Michelago to help load Frosty and I onto the float, and then she hopped in her ute and led the way since Chris didn't know where LYH was. As the float skimmed along down the highway, I started to feel very tired and unwell. I always sweated a lot when I was travelling and it was so hot and stuffy in the float; usually there was fresh air rushing in over my rump but in this float there was a heavy canvas awning on the back that had been rolled down so we were completely closed in. Sweat was trickling down my face and foaming up on my chest as I swayed and staggered, trying to keep my balance during the seemingly never-ending drive. My head was spinning and I could barely open my eyes. I could feel all my muscles starting to burn from the effort of keeping me standing and my legs were trembling underneath my own weight.

I felt the float beginning to slow down as we got to the edge of Canberra and we started to take a left turn. As I shifted and stumbled, leaning in the turning float, I knew I couldn't hold myself up anymore. I let out a terrified high-pitched squeal as my aching legs gave way underneath me and I crashed to the floor heavily, gasping for breath and struggling wildly to get up. I was on my side, stuck under the stallion divider in the middle of the float, and my legs were all tangled up with the legs of a very frightened and bewildered Frosty Jack. I thrashed and kicked and tried to surge forward, hoping I could get to my feet, but it was hopeless.

Frosty was looking down at me in horror, his eyes huge and wide and his nostrils flared as he snorted in distress. Luckily for me though, he didn't panic. If he had started to prance around and get upset, he could have fallen over too, or he could have stood on my legs and broken them. He was naturally a flighty, jumpy horse but somehow that day he knew that the best thing he could do was to stay absolutely still and wait for help.

It felt like it took hours to get to LYH. I laid there on the floor, bleeding and dirty, my heart pounding. My head and neck was jammed awkwardly against the wall of the float, with Frosty standing over me completely rigid. Every muscle in his body was tense and tight as he held himself still so that he wouldn't do any more damage to me. When the float finally stopped, I didn't even bother trying to get up; I knew I was well and truly stuck.

I heard the sound of Leanne's voice chatting away to Chris outside, and then the canvas awning covering the back of the float was unclipped and flicked up over the roof. Leanne was standing near the tailgate and with absolute horror she realised that she could only see one rump standing in the float, not 2. She ran to the side of the float and opened the access door near the front, and immediately burst into tears as she saw me lying there, bloodied and terrified. Frosty was dripping with sweat, his muscles still tensed rock hard and he was snorting loudly and sharply as he waited for someone to help us. The tailgate was lowered and Leanne and Chris stood there in shock, their eyes wide as they looked at the tangled mess of horse.

Frosty's back leg was jammed so tightly up against my flank that at first Leanne thought his leg had gone right through me; it was his bad leg and the friction of my flank against him had rubbed the top layer off his scar, causing it to bleed. Leanne spoke to me gently, telling me it was going to be ok and that they would get me out, but I could hear the fear in her voice and for a while I really thought that this was how I was going to die. Leanne was very worried that I might have broken legs or internal injuries, and it took a little while and a lot of help to come up with a plan to get Frosty and I out.

The first thing they needed to do was get Frosty out of the way so that they could get in and try to remove the stallion divider. That would be the only way I might be able to stand myself up. Otherwise the only other option would be to try to drag me out and no one was sure how they would manage to do that, especially without hurting me. Before they took Frosty out, they wrapped my legs up in anything they could find just in case Frosty stepped on me- they used towels, rugs, blankets and jumpers, many of which were borrowed from startled onlookers' cars. Once my legs were wrapped up to protect them, Chris untied Frosty and they started to slowly, carefully, back him off the float. He was so scared that he didn't want to move, so Leanne had to help him by picking up one of his feet at a time and gently placing it where he needed to stand. One by one, she lifted his hooves and helped him step back, until finally he was down the ramp and out of the float. He was trembling all over, exhausted and distressed, and I wished so desperately that I could have been out too. My ordeal was not yet over.

Once Frosty was unloaded, a kind stranger led him to a yard and gave him a drink and a biscuit of hay while Leanne and Chris worked on removing the stallion divider from inside the float. Some of it came apart and could be taken out easily, but because of where my head and neck were, the whole internal structure of the float needed to be unbolted and removed, piece by piece. Someone had raced down to the manager's house to fetch Barry, and he hurried to grab some tools and come up to the parking area where a crowd had gathered and were watching on anxiously.

Leanne crouched in the float beside me and patted me gently, speaking to me quietly and trying to keep me calm while Barry undid bolts and slowly pulled the rest of the divider out. Then it was time to see if I could get up. Everything had been removed, there was no longer any metal frames in my way and the only thing that was stopping me from standing myself up was the narrowness of the space I had, and the sheer exhaustion I was feeling. Leanne had already called the vet, letting them know what had happened and asking them to come out urgently to check me over once they got me out. Someone was on their way, and now it was up to me to get myself out of this awful oversize tin can I was trapped in.

Leanne tugged gently on my lead rope, guiding my head around to face the tailgate where she was standing, and I mustered every ounce of strength I had left and tried desperately to get to my feet. My front legs were stretched out in front of me and my back legs were curled underneath me but I was so tired and in so much pain that I just couldn't do it. I couldn't stand up. Leanne let me rest for a few minutes, and when my aching muscles stopped trembling she urged me to try again. This went on and on, so many failed attempts, so much fading hope. I kept trying, wanting so badly to find the strength to get to my feet and walk out of the float. I leaned back against the cold metal wall behind me to catch my breath, and as I laid there, a series of memories started racing through my mind. There I was, standing in the paddock at Hall seeing a 14-year old Leanne for the first time. Sailing happily over jumps at Macarthur with Leanne young and laughing on my back. Riding through the fragrant pine trees on our way to have a picnic, trotting along at the gymkhana with my bright pink hairspray, splashing in the dam with Kaz and Jake. I saw Moppy and Billy and Max, my dear friends that I missed so much. The happiest days of my life played like an old-time movie in my head and I suddenly felt a burst of energy, an intense longing to get up and get on with the next chapter of my life. My story would not finish here in this dirty smelly old float!

With all of my strength, I heaved myself forward and Leanne pulled with all her might on my lead rope. Every muscle in my worn-out old body screamed with pain but I pushed as hard as I could and with one final surge forward, I rose triumphantly to my feet. I was standing! The crowd cheered and several of the women were crying, overwhelmed with emotion as I slowly, painfully limped down the ramp onto solid ground. I was out!

The vet arrived shortly after that and checked me over. I had a lot of painful grazes where I'd been lying and thrashing around on the harsh rubber matting of the float floor. I was also very muscle-sore and tired, and the hock that I'd broken a few years earlier was very swollen. By some miracle though, there were no obvious serious injuries so the vet gave me some pain relief and anti-inflammatories and told Leanne to call them if the swelling on my hock didn't go away after a couple of days. What a terrible ordeal. I hoped I'd never see another horse float again in my life.

We hadn't been able to get me a place in a stable yet, so Leanne slowly led me over to the paddock I would be staying in for a while. Frosty was waiting for me, still wide-eyed and worried, and he nuzzled me with concern as I limped slowly through the gate. Leanne made me a feed but I was too tired to eat; my pain-killers had kicked in by then so I dropped down onto the soft grass, sighed gently through my nostrils, then I closed my eyes and fell into a deep sleep.

Chapter 18 – No longer seeing things clearly

Things at LYH hadn't really changed too much since I'd left, and I really was happy to be back. It only took a couple of weeks for a stable to become available, and I was so excited to walk back into the familiar old breezeway. My hooves clip-clopped loudly on the concrete floor and I breathed in the smell of fresh sawdust as I entered my new stable. Leanne had already hung up a hay net stuffed with lucerne for me, my water trough was sparkling clean and my rugs were hanging up ready to be put on for my first night in. It was like I had stepped straight back in time, into my happy earlier life before we'd moved away. I was recovering well after the awful incident in the float, and it felt like things were falling back into place for us now that Leanne had finally walked away from the pain and stress of the life she had been living with Liam.

Some horses had left LYH while I was gone and new ones had moved in, but there were still lots of horses in the stable block that I knew from before. There was one grumpy old gelding that I remembered, but I didn't particularly like him. He was a very dark bay with a narrow white blaze on his head and his name was Bob. He was very bad-tempered and he always glared and pinned his ears back angrily at every single horse who walked past his stable. He was right in the middle of the block so it wasn't like we could avoid going near him! I just tried to stay out of his way as much as I could... that is until I got put into the same day paddock as him.

Just like a couple of years earlier when I'd been paired up with Jess the bullying stockhorse, neither myself nor Leanne was happy at all when Barry decided Bob and I would be paddock-mates. I was getting older, I'd been through so much in the last few years, and Leanne was worried that Bob might attack me and hurt me. Well I'm very sorry to say that she was right to be worried, because that's exactly what happened.

At first I managed to avoid getting too close to the cranky old nag I was stuck in the paddock with. I tried to be positive and I told myself it was only during the day, and at least I'd be safe and sound every night when I went to bed in my lovely warm stable away from him. Unfortunately for me, Bob seemed to get more and more annoyed by my presence as the days went on, and he started to come after me no matter how hard I tried to keep out of his way. He would see me from across the paddock and come storming over to chase me and bite me, and he would squeal and bare his teeth and roll his eyes back in his head like some sort of terrifying devil horse! I started to feel very nervous every morning knowing I would once again spend all my time running away from him. Sometimes when it was raining I'd be overjoyed because I knew Leanne might decide to keep me inside for the day and just leave my back stable door open so I could use my little yard.

One afternoon I was dozing peacefully in the furthest corner of the paddock, minding my own business and trying to stay out of sight, when suddenly SMACK, something smashed into the side of my face so hard I felt instantly dizzy and sick. I took off running, confused and disoriented about what had just happened, and as I ran I looked behind me and there was Bob. He was prancing and pigrooting angrily and swishing his tail as he glared menacingly at me, and I suddenly realised what had happened. That nasty miserable bully had just kicked me in the head while I was asleep! The side of my face was stinging unbearably, throbbing deep into my skull and I could feel my eye closing over as it started to swell. I snorted in distress and was horrified to feel warm blood trickling out of one nostril. Bob had already wandered arrogantly away and was grazing as if nothing had happened, and I spent the rest of the afternoon fearfully trying to keep out of his sight in case he attacked me again.

By the time Leanne arrived in the evening to bring

me in for the night, the throbbing in my head had eased off and I was feeling a little bit better. The kick to the face had taken me by surprise and it had really hurt at the time, but I was relieved that perhaps it wasn't that serious after all. It had left a split just under my eye which was small but deep, and there was still a fair bit of swelling but it wasn't bad enough for Leanne to notice right away. She led me into my stable and as she undid my halter and hung it up she spotted the cut and realised that I looked puffy around my eye and down the side of my face. She frowned as she had a closer look and recognised the familiar type of graze a kick from a horse's hoof leaves, then she glanced over at Bob's stable and shook her head with frustration. It was hard to find a good paddock mate, why were horses always so temperamental and grumpy?

Because the little cut below my eyelid appeared to be pretty minor at that stage, Leanne decided to wait and see how it looked in the morning. She brought me my feed and hay, rugged me and gave me a goodnight cuddle, and headed home for the night. I munched happily on my dinner, feeling calm and relaxed, and after a while I drifted off to sleep.

Very early the next morning, I was woken by a very unpleasant dull ache in the side of my head. I opened my eyes and was surprised to discover that my off-side eye, the side that I'd been kicked on, was very sore and starting to swell up again. When Leanne arrived at about 8:00 she noticed it straight away and decided to keep me in for the day, which suited me just fine. As hours passed, my face started to throb and by afternoon I was really in a lot of pain. Leanne came up that evening earlier than usual to see how I was going, and she seemed very worried. It must have looked bad because she got on the phone to my old familiar friend the vet and started telling them what was going on. They were very busy and told her to give me some bute for the inflammation, keep monitoring it and if it hadn't improved or was worse by the following morning to ring back and they would send someone out.

I had a terrible night that night. The pain got worse and worse, throbbing and aching, and I felt hot and clammy and miserable. By the time the sun was rising, I couldn't even open my eye anymore; it had swollen up so much it had closed over. I paced back and forth in my stable, feeling irritated and restless from the pain. It felt very strange and unpleasant not being able to see on one side and it made me feel very anxious. Leanne walked up to my stable when she got there, took one look at me and gasped in horror.

The whole side of my face had blown up like a balloon, I could barely breathe through that nostril and my poor eye was hidden under all the hot burning swelling. She called the vet and told them it was urgent, and thankfully within the hour someone arrived to see me. They poked and prodded my poor face and I was in so much pain that I swished my tail, stomped my front foot angrily and kept trying to back away and escape from them, which was very unlike my usual calm self. After the painful examination the vet told Leanne that, as she had already suspected, there was a nasty infection going on in the tissue around my eye and I would need to start a course of strong antibiotics straight away. They gave me some needles; one for pain, one for inflammation and one to get the antibiotic treatment started. Then the vet handed Leanne a stack of needles and syringes and some bottles of medicine for her to continue treating me with. As the drugs started to kick in and the awful pain subsided, I felt so relieved that I wanted to canter around my paddock and kick up my heels! That would not be an option however, because I was to be confined to my stable for the next few days at least.

It took about 24 hours for the swelling and inflammation around my eye to go down, and when I woke up early the next morning I started to work on getting my poor eyelid to unstick and open up. The infection seemed to be almost under control now, it was going away almost as quickly as it had come on, and I very gently and carefully rubbed my eye on my front leg to loosen it up. After a couple of minutes, it worked and I felt my top and bottom eyelid unstick from each other and slowly open. I was expecting things to be a little bit blurry at first since it had been closed for quite a while, but nothing prepared me for what I actually saw as I rose my head and tried to look around...

Black. There was nothing. My near-side eye could see everything; my stable, my feed bucket, the rake leaning against the wall in the breezeway. But my offside eye... it was wide open, and I saw absolutely nothing. I tried not to panic but the unrelenting blackness made me feel claustrophobic and unbalanced. I shook my head violently, my breath rasping loudly in and out of my lungs as I desperately rubbed the eye on my leg again and again and tried to look around. I kept hoping that it would change but it stayed the same – I couldn't see anything, one whole side of my world was plunged into a permanent empty darkness. My heart was pounding loudly in my ears and I felt sick as I realised that my vision had gone... I was half blind.

While I was immediately aware of what had happened, it took Leanne a little while to realise that I could no longer see out of the injured eye. The infection that had caused the damage cleared up and I was allowed to go back out during the day. I would be getting a new paddock mate of course, because Leanne refused to put me in with Bob ever again.

About a week later, Leanne arrived late in the afternoon as usual to bring me in for the night and get my feed ready. I was standing in the shade looking out at the hills and enjoying the fresh evening breeze, and Leanne came walking up towards me on my off side. She had called out to me as she approached but I was getting old and my hearing wasn't very good so I hadn't heard a thing. Because I was awake and alert, Leanne had assumed that I could see her and she walked straight up to me and went to greet me with a pat on the neck. The second that I felt her touch me, I got the fright of my life. I jumped and shied violently, a shrill squeal escaped from my throat and I started to run away, my primal equine instincts exploding with fear that a predator was after me. As I took off, I glanced around to see what had happened and there was Leanne standing there, a surprised and shocked expression on her face as she wondered why I was behaving in such a way. I pranced and snorted, tossing my head at her as if to say 'don't scare me like that!' and then wandered back over to her to eat my carrot. She put my halter on slowly, and then she stood directly in front of me and leaned in to look at my eyes. On my near side, she carefully pointed a finger towards my eye as if she was going to poke it, to see what I would do. I blinked and moved my head away to avoid getting poked, and then she turned her attention to the off side where I'd had the kick and then the infection. This time when she moved her finger towards my eye, I couldn't see it so I didn't blink, and I didn't try to move away. I just stood there. When she realised that I could no longer see from the injured eye, she gasped and covered her mouth with her hand. She stood there for a minute, looking at me with tears in her eyes, then she carefully walked in front of me and went to stand on my good side where she knew I could see her. She gently clicked her tongue at me to let me know we were going to walk, and we wandered slowly back to my stable together. I felt relieved that she finally knew what had happened, and grateful that she was going to help me manage it.

From that moment on, Leanne always made sure that she approached me on my near side so as not to startle me. If she was doing something on my blind side, such as putting my rug on or picking out my feet, she would run her hand along my side and keep talking to me the whole time so that I could keep one ear on her and know where she was. As time went on I started to adapt and get used to only having vision on one side. It still brought many challenges to my life though, and I felt lucky to have a safe place to live and a best friend to help me get through the most difficult days, no matter what.

Chapter 19 – Perfect and imperfect moments

Life had gotten a little bit harder for me but it was still very peaceful and relaxing. I continued to enjoy living in my stable, and best of all Barry let me have my day paddock all to myself once he found out I had lost the vision in my injured eye. I no longer had to worry about another horse sneaking up on my bad side to bite my spotted rump or unkindly chase me away from the water trough, and I was very grateful for that. There was one thing that I really missed though- since the day she'd realised I'd gone half-blind, Leanne hadn't taken me out for a single ride.

I guess she thought it would be too hard for me to go out on the trail when I couldn't see properly, so I had basically been retired. I was getting old, there was no doubt about that, but I was still healthy and strong and I wanted to get out! I loved the comfort and safety of my stable but my soul yearned for wide open spaces. I wanted to canter along bush trails, I wanted to feel the wind in my mane, and inhale the intoxicating scent of eucalyptus leaves and pine needles, and watch the sun setting from a hill high above the horizon. I needed to feel a little bit of freedom and excitement in these old bones of mine!

A few months later, the day I'd been longing for finally arrived. Leanne turned up at around the usual time late in the afternoon, but instead of making my dinner and putting my rugs on, she started brushing me and picking out my feet. Could it be? Could we actually be getting out of here for a while and going on an adventure? Leanne wandered out of my stable and disappeared for a few minutes, and while I waited for her to come back I hoped and hoped that she wouldn't just walk back in with my feed bucket. It must have been my lucky day, because when Leanne came back she was carrying my saddle on her hip and had my bridle over her shoulder.

Hooray! I flared my nostrils and pushed my ears as far forward as they could possibly go, I was so happy. We were going for a ride! As Leanne saddled me up, she chattered away to me about how she'd been thinking it was time she tried taking me out to see how I handled being ridden now that I was blind in one eye. She was pretty confident that I would be alright, because she knew that I trusted her and she knew that she could trust me too. As she led me out of the breezeway and into the cool open air, I sighed happily and stood patiently while she hopped up onto my back. She gathered up my reins, clapped me affectionately on the neck with her hand, and said 'come on girl, let's go', and we headed off towards the front gate that would take us out into the world. It was quite late in the afternoon as we made our way around the base of the hill that stood beside LYH. The sun was starting to set and shades of pastel pinks and oranges were creeping up from behind the distant mountains, flooding the sky with colour. Our shadows stretched out beside us as we wandered through the fading light, casting a comical silhouette that made us look 10 feet tall. A large mob of cockatoos were screeching at each other as they flew in circles high above us, and up ahead I saw a small brown rabbit dart off into the bushes, his fluffy white tail bobbing as he scampered out of our way. Leanne had been worried at first, unsure of how I would manage my partial blindness, but it hadn't taken her long to realise that I was just as happy to be out for a ride as she was.

We walked slowly, relaxed and content, enjoying each other's company in the gentle evening breeze. At one point there was an uphill section of the trail that was grassy and clear of rocks, and Leanne squeezed her heels to my sides and loosened the reins, letting me know I could speed up. I started to jog, then within a few steps I broke into a canter and we sailed along the track together, feeling free and serene, all the way to the top of the slope. It was starting to get dark by then so Leanne pressed one rein against my neck and turned me towards home. We walked along, Leanne holding my reins loosely in one hand, her body swaying gently in rhythm with each step that I took, and we both listened to the sounds of the bush coming to life around us. Crickets were chirping in the ground beneath my feet, gum leaves rustled gently in the breeze, and somewhere off in the distance a kookaburra was cackling a cheerful farewell to the last streaks of daylight holding on above the horizon. It really was a perfect ride, and that was a perfect moment.

When we got back to the stables it was dark, and all of the cars had gone from in front of the stable block except for Leanne's. It seemed fitting that we had the place to ourselves now; after such a tranquil evening ride it wouldn't have felt right to walk in to the usual hustle and bustle of the afternoon feeding rush. Leanne undid my girth and slid the saddle from my back, placing it gently into the tray of her ute. Then she led me to my stable, gave me a quick brush with my favourite soft body brush, then she went to mix up my dinner. I chewed it slowly, relishing the sweet taste of the fresh lucerne chaff and delicious molasses-covered grain mix, as Leanne put my night time rugs on and made sure everything in my stable was clean and ready for me. She barely spoke as she went about her routine; there was no need for words tonight. The feeling of contentment and serenity between us was palpable; I don't think either of us had ever felt more grounded and at peace with our world. It will always be one of my favourite memories.

A few months after our perfect evening ride, Leanne invited one of her friends out to LYH to go for a ride. His name was Josh and he used to have horses when he was younger so he wasn't too bad in the saddle. The plan was that Leanne was going to ride Frosty, and Josh was going to ride me, because I was quieter and he hadn't ridden in a few years. They were going to meet out the front of the stables, but Leanne had to get Frosty first so she drove to the back of LYH to the sprawling shady paddock she was leasing for him. She groomed him, saddled him up, mounted and started riding him towards the stables. From my yard I could see them making their way down the dirt road; Frosty was jogging along quite quickly, and Leanne was sitting to the trot in her black western saddle, with the reins in one hand and a spare girth for Josh to use in the other.

Now Frosty was quite a flighty spirited horse with a tendency to shy at things with no warning, so I was surprised that Leanne was so relaxed. She usually needed to keep him reined in and be on high alert in case an invisible horse-eating gremlin jumped out and spooked him. It was as if Frosty could read my mind, because one minute they were trotting down the road beautifully, and the next everything suddenly went out of control. To this day I still don't really know whether something frightened him or he was just being naughty, but out of nowhere the shining, muscular chestnut suddenly launched himself forward in a wild cat leap, and then kicked up his heels and did a violent and very powerful buck. Leanne had been completely unprepared for such a thing, and the force of the buck threw her forward out of the saddle and onto Frosty's withers. She had dropped the girth she'd been holding and was now hanging onto his neck as she tried to regain control of the crazed gelding who had seemed so calm only moments earlier. Within a second Frosty decided it was time to bail out, and once again in a completely unexpected move he spun around on his heels and started to gallop off. As he spun, Leanne was thrown from her awkward position on his neck and she landed on her knees in the grass at the edge of the road. Frosty must have thought he was home free when he tried to take off, he looked very excited and pleased with himself as he did it. Unfortunately for both of them, Leanne was still gripping the reins tightly in her hand from her landing place on the ground and when he tried to run off she hung on! The tension of the reins snapped his silly snorting head back around towards her and the force of it almost dislocated Leanne's shoulder, but she managed to hang on and stop him from bolting off down the road.

She must have been hurting from both the fall and the enormous tug on her shoulder, but if she was she didn't show it. As I watched the scene unfolding down on the road below, I was shocked that Frosty could be so naughty. I thought I'd played up for Leanne a few times but oh boy, it was never anything like this! Thank goodness he hadn't thrown out a kick from his back leg when he tried to spin around and run away, because if he did it would have hit Leanne square in the face and could have killed her. The hairs along my spine had been standing on end and I'd felt like I could hardly breathe as I'd watched in horror.

Leanne had gotten to her feet now, still holding on tightly to the reins of the wild Frosty Jack, who really seemed to have lost his mind. I could see by the way she approached him that she was seriously cranky. As she stormed furiously towards him, Frosty retreated, pigrooting and threatening to rear as he continued to dance on the end of his reins. She roared at him to stand up, and this confirmed for me that she was angry because it was so loud that I could hear it from my stable as clear as a bell. Frosty looked so startled that the tips of his ears almost met in the middle, and even though he was still very fired up and over-excited, he decided that he should probably stand still for a second. I had a quiet giggle to myself as she yelled at him, waving her arms and demanding to know what his problem was and why he had carried on like that. He attempted another little dance and snorted wildly, rolling his eyes and tossing his head as he pranced on the spot, but Leanne was having none of it. She roared at him again to stand, and then she marched over to pick up the spare girth that she had dropped, dragging the silly cavorting horse along behind her. She had dirt and grass stains all over the knees of her jeans and she kept putting her hand on her injured shoulder, but she was so angry with Frosty for his behaviour that she climbed back onto his back anyway. It reminded me of that time years ago when I shied and stood on the back of her ankle, and she was so cross with me that even though she was hurt she made me go for a ride anyway. It was good to see her stubbornness hadn't faded as she'd grown up, I thought to myself and snorted in amusement.

By this stage Leanne had managed, with some difficulty, to get onto Frosty's back again, but this time there was no one-handed relaxed jog; she kept him tightly reined in and gave him a firm no-nonsense kick with her heels to tell him to walk on. I could see from the tense, tucked-up way Frosty walked and the way he kept tossing his head against his bit that he was by no means finished with his performance just yet, and I was right.

Josh arrived at the stables, and he held Frosty while Leanne saddled me up. Frosty kept eyeballing him with a wild stare that reminded me of how Billy the goat used to look at me when he was in a crazy mood. Once I was ready, Leanne led me outside, they both mounted and we started walking towards the front gate. It was a little bit windy that day, which usually puts horses in a silly mood; we get worried that we won't hear the horse-eating monsters creeping up on us from behind every tree and rock we go past. I was made even more anxious by the agitated energy I could sense coming from Frosty. He was still a big shiny chestnut ball of nervous energy, just waiting to go off, and he was about to get his chance.

We had only walked about 200 metres from the front entrance to LYH, heading towards the river that snaked its way through the valley below the mountains at the end of the road. On the right side of us was the boundary fence of LYH, and on the left side was lots of long dead grass and some messy little native shrubs and trees. I had just been thinking to myself how it would be easy for a gremlin to hide amongst it, when suddenly... WHOOSH! Out of that scary long grass exploded a terrifying, enormous, hairy nasty horse-eating monster! Petrified, I did a crazed lunge away from the hideous creature and my heart pounded so hard and so fast that I thought it might beat right out of my chest! A high-pitched squeal came from deep down in my throat and in that split second I was certain that I was about to die, eaten by the horrible monster that had just ambushed us as we walked past its lair. Josh was pulling hard on my reins and struggling to calm me down and stay on my back, but compared to what Leanne was dealing with, his problems were minor!

Frosty had absolutely lost the plot. He had already been on the verge of snapping, and now he had exploded just as violently as the monster when it had come bursting out of the grass. It happened so quickly but it somehow seemed to be in slow motion at the same time; the monster rushed out of its lair directly in front of Frosty, so close that it almost crashed straight into him. He was instantly completely out of control, his mind overtaken by the self-preservation instincts of his equine brain firing the same message to him, over and over: RUN, RUN, RUN! He was no longer able to contain himself and he was also no longer aware of Leanne's presence on his back. He roared loudly, and it was a sound created by pure terror. The whites of his eyes were showing as they rolled back in his head, and then he did an almighty rear up onto his back legs, spun around, and he bolted. There was no chance of Leanne calming him down, all she could do was hold on for dear life and hope that he would stop before they went through a fence or galloped in front of a car. As he took off, they passed by me so close that I could feel the rush of air they'd created and I got a brief glimpse of Leanne's surprised expression as they thundered back along the path towards the front gate of LYH.

Thankfully Frosty wasn't particularly fit at the time, and his crazed gallop came to a stop right in the middle of the front gateway. His sides were heaving up and down as he struggled to catch his breath, exhausted, and his chest and flanks were foamed up with sweat. Josh had started trotting me back towards them and I was so relieved to see that the moronic horse had stopped before anything bad had happened. Frosty seemed to have gotten his silly mood out of his system by then, and after a few minutes of calming-down time we did end up continuing our

I STILL DREAM OF HORSES

ride.

Ok, ok, I know. You want to know what happened to the ferocious beast that viciously attacked us and caused Frosty to bolt. Look, I'm blind in one eye and my hearing isn't very good so don't make fun of me. It wasn't ACTUALLY a monster. It was a big, frightened and very elderly-looking kangaroo which had been taking a quiet nap in the grass, and we must have startled it just as much as it startled us. He did come bursting suddenly out of the grass, and it was very scary, but he very quickly took off and hopped away from us as fast as he could. It seemed like certain death to Frosty and I at first, but once I calmed down and got a better look at the fearsome 'monster' as he fled the scene, I saw that he was in pretty rough condition and probably would have had trouble eating a gum leaf let alone a fully-grown horse!

It was a little bit embarrassing for both of us horses and we agreed never to speak of the scary kangaroo again. Frosty didn't keep his end of the bargain though, because one time I overheard him telling the mares that lived next door to him about the day he bravely rescued us all from a huge frightening beast that lurked in the grass outside our boundary fence. I couldn't believe what I was hearing and I pinned my ears back and tossed my head at him as if to say 'get real you clown!', but the handsome cheeky gelding just winked at me and kept telling his story. Oh well, it was entertaining and it gave me a good laugh if nothing else.

Chapter 20 – Back to the country life

The months rolled by happily at LYH; it was now 2007 and I was enjoying being back in my comfortable, settled stabled life. Every afternoon as I would head in from my day paddock to the stable block I would look out over the hills and take in the stunning scenery of mountainous bushland and native birds in flight. I was around 30 years old by then, and as the seasons continued to change in the world around me I was aware that the seasons were also changing within me. I had lived through so many hot, dry bushfire summers, glorious emerald green flower-dotted springtimes, crisp blue-skied autumns that swirled with crunchy orange leaves, and icy cold winters that made the grass too frozen to eat in the early mornings. Things were certainly slowing down for me; my body was getting tired, sometimes I ached for no real reason, and I was happy to spend my days relaxing in the paddock on my own, dozing in the sun and swatting away the occasional pesky fly with my tail. I knew I was heading into the sunset years of my life, but I was healthy, I was happy and I was very loved so I didn't put too much thought into it. I knew I had a few good years still left in me yet!

One chilly winter morning Leanne turned up and came walking into the breezeway just like every other day, her boots echoing on the cold concrete as she approached my stable. Nothing was different about her arrival that day, but I just had a feeling that she was going to tell me something big. We knew each other so well that I could sense it from the moment I heard her. I felt a knot tightening in my stomach as she opened the door, and I wasn't in the least bit surprised when she said 'I've got some news for you!'

As she started undoing my warm winter rugs to take them off for the day, she told me that she was moving in with her boyfriend, Greg, who she had been seeing for about a year. Ok, I thought, so what's that got to do with me? Then she dropped the bomb. They were moving in together in Yass, the town where Greg was from! Yass was about an hour's drive away, and at first I was thinking to myself that she was going to be spending a lot of time and fuel driving back and forth from Yass to Canberra to see me every day. But then she started talking about paying someone to transport me by truck rather than risk putting me in a float again, and I realised that it wasn't just her that was moving to Yass. I was going too, and Frosty!

Never mind the knot, it felt like my whole stomach dropped out of me completely. I couldn't believe it,

I loved my stabled life and my private paddock, I thought we were happy here, and now she was moving me again. I was so cross and upset with her that I pinned my ears back and sulked all the way to my paddock when she led me out. My bottom lip hung down loosely, twitching with sadness, and my mind swirled with unhappy thoughts of having to uproot and relocate again. I was too old to keep packing up and leaving my home!

A couple of weeks later, the time had come; we were leaving. Leanne took all of my gear and feed out of the tack room and packed it into the back of her ute, then she turned her attention to me. She swapped my toasty warm rugs for a cool lightweight summer sheet, she carefully encased my tail in a thick bandage, and she had even bought huge thick protective float boots to put on me to protect my legs while I was on the truck. After what had happened when I fell in the float last time I guess she didn't want to take too many chances. By the time she had finished getting me ready, I felt like one of those American gridiron players covered in padding and safety gear! The long puffy boots made it hard to walk and Leanne giggled at me as I goose-stepped down the breezeway with wild over-exaggerated movements.

Frosty was standing outside the stables with his fat head buried in a bucket of feed Leanne had given him to keep him entertained while we waited, and he looked very flashy in his white cotton rug and red float boots that matched his cheerful bright red halter. I didn't feel flashy at all in my protective get-up, I felt ridiculous, and I snorted unhappily at Leanne to let her know I was displeased! In the distance I heard the faint rumbling of a large diesel engine, and a minute later the truck Leanne had booked came driving up the road to collect us. I didn't want to leave, but I was too old to put up a fight and it wouldn't have changed things anyway. Feeling completely downtrodden, I watched in despair as Frosty was loaded onto the truck, and then it was my turn. Leanne had told the driver that I was blind on one side and had fallen last time I was transported, so the kindly gentleman was very nice to me and helped Leanne walk me slowly up the ramp. Once I was on board, he told Leanne that it was probably better if they put me in the end bay of the truck, and left me untied so that I could move around and balance myself if I needed to. It would also be better if I wasn't tied up just in case I fell again; if I was down and had my head tied awkwardly to the side wall of the truck it could make a bad situation even worse. Leanne looked very worried but she put her faith in the driver, who seemed to be very experienced and knowledgeable, and agreed to leave me untied. She gave Frosty and I a big cuddle and a loving pat on the face and told us she would see us when we got to Yass. A protective bar with a large piece of black rubber matting hanging from it was pushed across to give me an enclosed space to travel in, and the heavy tailgate closed behind us. Here we go again, I sighed to myself sadly. It was really happening.

I'm very relieved to tell you that the journey to our new home actually went very well. Unlike the stuffy float I'd collapsed in last time we moved, the truck had high windows running right along the length of each side so there was a continuous stream of fresh cool air coming in. I had plenty of room to move about, and the driver took each twist and turn in the road very slowly and carefully. When we finally got to our destination, a picturesque sprawling property on Wargeila Road just out of Yass, the tailgate was lowered and as I blinked in the bright afternoon sunlight, I saw Leanne standing there with my lead rope in her hand waiting to greet us. Even though I was mad at her, I was so relieved to have had a good trip that I whinnied to her and she said 'hello baby girl!' as she strode up the ramp towards me.

Frosty and I were unloaded and put in a large yard to wait while Leanne gratefully thanked the truck driver and paid him for his excellent service, and then he closed the tailgate and drove away. Leanne came wandering over and asked us what we thought of our new paddock, and as I looked around I had to admit it was very pretty. It must have been about 50 acres, and it was a lovely fragrant mixture of bushland flats and grassy rolling hills. In the middle of the property there was a beautiful rustic-looking hayshed that looked like it could have been a blacksmith's headquarters a hundred years ago, and tucked away down on the far fence line was a pretty little cottage surrounded by a garden that was bursting with flowers of every colour and lots of arty-looking sculptures and statues. I was disappointed that there were no stables, but I couldn't deny the whole place had a very welcoming and relaxed feel about it. Frosty, however, was not picking up on the tranquility vibe and was pacing up and down the edge of the yard, snorting and tossing his head and prancing. His muscles twitched anxiously beneath his bright chestnut coat, and I was just about to tell him to settle down when he suddenly stood up tall and proud and let out an ear-piercingly loud neigh that seemed to reverberate right through the peaceful valley of our new home.

Off in the distance I heard a faint whinny of reply travelling along the breeze towards us. My ears snapped forward and I raised my head and looked in the direction it had come from. Unsure if I was hearing things, I waited, and sure enough a moment later I heard it again. There were other horses here! I turned towards Leanne and tossed my head at her unhappily. She hadn't told me this was going to be a shared arrangement! Now I would have to put up with other horses picking on me and beating me up just like in my younger days at Macarthur Park. Within seconds I could hear hoofbeats thundering towards us and a mob of horses appeared over the crest of the hill. There was about 8 of them, mostly just ordinary-looking chestnuts and bays... but then I caught sight of something that made my heart skip a beat.

Bumbling along awkwardly behind the rest of the herd came a huge hairy figure, an enormous heavy horse with fluff-covered feet and a big white face. My breath caught in my throat and I could hardly breathe as I watched the familiar shape drawing closer... MOPPY!

There he was, my dear gentle beautiful old friend that I had missed so dearly. No other horse could possibly have that same massive head and huge fluffy legs like he did! I called out to him, a happy jingling whinny that was filled with pure joy and excitement to see my special friend again. What was he doing out here? I had so many questions for him, I couldn't wait to catch up and find out all about what he had been doing for the last couple of years!

He hadn't answered me so I paced along the fence impatiently and whinnied to him again, bursting with happiness and eager for him to recognise me. He had slowed from his trotting and was walking now, and as he got closer I stopped pacing and stood still, staring at him. I was confused; his coat looked lighter than I remembered. Moppy's coat before had been a rich red with occasional patches of roan flecked through it, but looking at him now his coat was almost all roan and it was much paler than it used to be. He kept walking closer with the rest of the herd, until he was only about 10 metres from where I stood, and as I got a better look at him my heart sank. The horse standing before me was most certainly a clydesdale... but it wasn't Moppy.

I felt tears welling up in my eyes as the realisation hit me. I had been absolutely overjoyed to see my dear old friend, but this horse standing here in front of me was a stranger. In fact, it wasn't even a gelding, it was a mare. Just like Moppy, she had a large white blaze down the length of her face and she had the unmistakable fluffy white feathers of a clydie, but that was where the similarities stopped. Her coat was a pale strawberry roan, her mane wasn't as long and thick as Moppy's, and under her forelock she didn't have the same enormous gentle eyes I had come to know and love. I didn't want to accept it but I had no choice... It wasn't him.

I don't think I have ever felt as heartbroken and disappointed as I did in that moment. I slowly lowered my head, sighed deeply through my nostrils and pinned my ears back sadly. The strange clydesdale mare looked at me with disinterest then turned away and started grazing, unaware of the agonising hurt she had just caused me. It wasn't her fault I'd mistaken her for someone else, but I felt so overwhelmed by my disappointment that I couldn't even look at her. I'd only ever seen one clydesdale in real life before, which was Moppy, and I was so shocked to see another one and discover it wasn't my special friend. At this time, when we had all moved to Yass, Moppy was with his new owners, he was still alive and as far as we knew he was living in agistment on the outskirts of Canberra so there was every chance that it could have been him. Alas, it wasn't, and I never did get to see my gentle Moppy again.

Most of the horses we shared our new home with at Yass were fairly anti-social and not at all interested in making friends with us. I didn't really care; I was too busy trying to acquaint myself with my new surroundings to worry about making friends. Because I could only see one side of things, it was difficult for me to get my bearings and become familiar with the layout of the property. Frosty was no help; he'd taken a liking to one of the mares there and spent all of his time trying to impress her, prancing around and showing off like he was still a stallion.

Most of the time my vision didn't cause too many problems, I just had to have a good look around to make sure I was safe before I chose a spot to graze or to sleep. The one thing that I had constant trouble with was crossing the creek that flowed right through the middle of our paddock. It wasn't very deep at all; a horse could easily wade through it and barely get their hocks wet in most places. The problem was that it had very steep sides along most of its edge, and the easiest way to get across it was to use the concrete crossing that had been built for vehicles to drive over. Seems straightforward right? There's a crossing, so I should just use that and there won't be a problem. Unfortunately, no. The crossing was a big problem for me.

It was fairly wide and looked very strong, but whenever I tried to walk across it, I got so frightened that
most of the time I would back up and decide not to
try to walk over it. You see, when I was standing on it,
all I could see through my one good eye was the sheer
drop off the side of the crossing down into the freezing cold water below. Because I couldn't see out of my
other eye, I had no idea how close I was to the other
edge and I felt as if I was going to fall right over the
side. To try to see where I was going, every time I took
a step I had to keep stopping and spinning all the way
around in a full circle to get a view of both edges of
the crossing, and it took me several stressful minutes
every time I needed to get across.

One day I looked up from the patch of tasty grass I'd
been grazing on and realised that the rest of the herd
was way over the other side of the paddock. I didn't
want to be on my own, so I started walking towards
them but of course to get there I would have to get
over the dreaded creek crossing. My hooves made a
hollow echoey clip-clop sound as I stepped onto the
concrete, and immediately I was disorientated and
had to turn in a full circle to check if I was too close
to the side. So far so good, so I took another step forward. Once again I felt frightened of falling and had to
spin around to see where I was.

I was concentrating very hard, both on trying not

to fall off the crossing and trying not to get dizzy from spinning around, when I heard a soft friendly whinny and the sound of gentle hoof steps behind me. I looked around to see who was there, and I was surprised to see that it was Pony. Pony was a very tall and very old gelding who lived on the property with us. He looked like he might have been a showjumper or a fancy dressage horse in his younger years, but these days in his old age he was very slow-moving and easy going. His fading chestnut coat was flecked with white hairs, especially around his eyes and muzzle, and his wise friendly eyes were slightly cloudy when the sun shined into them.

Pony had been quietly watching me from a distance as I struggled to negotiate the concrete crossing, and when I heard him whinny and turned to look at him he started walking towards me. If it was any other horse I would have felt defensive and threatened, but I didn't feel like I needed to be afraid of Pony; he seemed like a very kindly old gentleman. He wandered up to me and offered me a friendly sniff, and I could sense that he meant no harm. He was here to help. From where he had been standing on my good side, he walked around behind me and moved up to stand beside me on my bad side where I couldn't see him. Then he took a step forward and butted me softly on the shoulder with his nose, gesturing that he wanted me to walk forward too. Hesitantly I lifted my front hoof and stepped forward. He nodded his big chestnut head, which had a narrow white stripe running down the length of his face, and whickered softly, letting me know I was doing well. He stepped forward again and I followed him, one step at a time, another then another, and in this way he slowly escorted me all the way to the other side of the crossing. Once we were safely off the concrete, I turned to face him and put my ears as far forward as I could get them. I was so grateful for the kindness he had showed me, and I softly touched my muzzle to his and snorted gently to say thank you.

While all of this was happening, I'd been so busy concentrating on the crossing that I hadn't seen Leanne's little blue ute pull up and park under the ghostly weeping old gum trees nearby. She had gotten there just in time to witness Pony's extraordinary gesture of kindness as he guided me over the creek, and she told me later that it was genuinely one of the most beautiful things she had ever had the good fortune of seeing. From that day on, she always made sure she had a few extra carrots for Pony when she came to feed Frosty and I, and she always gave him a pat and made sure he knew she appreciated his help.

Pony quickly became a very good, very special friend to me; he was never far away and any time that I felt lost or scared, all I had to do was whinny and within seconds he would appear at my side to help me get to where I needed to go. He was a very special gelding, and I will be forever grateful for the compassion and kindness he showed me in those days when we lived along the creek in the shadow of the silent old gum trees.

Chapter 21 – On the road of life again

The time that we spent on that pretty bush property out the back of Yass went by peacefully and uneventfully. The frosts and icy winds of winter blew themselves away, and the spring that followed was spent snoozing in the sunshine and getting fat pigging out on rich patches of sweet new grass. As summer rolled in, the usual annoying blowflies returned and the grass I had been enjoying so much died off and turned brittle and straw-like in the heat. Frosty's mare-crush he'd developed when we first got here hadn't worked out very well for him; he'd eventually had to swallow his pride and accept that despite his best attempts to impress her, she wasn't interested in him, and he had returned to grazing by my side every day along with my dear companion Pony. All 3 of us had become great friends; we spent the autumn together shying at the crunchy red and yellow leaves that fell from the deciduous trees in the house yard and floated over the fence, blowing through the paddock and dancing around at our feet. When the chilly winter winds came sneaking back in again the following year, we would huddle together amongst the trees and keep each other safe and warm, our breath rolling from our nostrils like smoke and mingling into a comforting misty cloud around our sleepy heads in the icy night air.

Those days at Yass weren't particularly exciting, and I don't really have any thrilling adventures to tell you all about; what I can tell you about them though, is that they were days spent in happiness, laziness, and contentment, and it was all thanks to the trust and friendship I shared with Frosty and Pony. Every after-noon Leanne would arrive after work to feed us and make sure we were alright, and I could see that she was very glad I had those loyal, lovely geldings to look out for me in my old age when she couldn't be around as much.

A little over a year after we first arrived at Yass, Leanne was offered a free paddock for us on a prop-erty she was working at in a small village called Book-ham. It was about half an hour away from Yass, and Leanne had been working there for several months. The property was on a shady, secluded eucalypt-lined road, and out there in what seemed like the middle of nowhere was a rose farm! It was a lovely place for Leanne to work, with several enormous greenhouses that each contained rows and rows of the most im-possibly beautiful roses in every colour you could imagine. At the start of every day, Leanne and her 2 bosses would walk up and down each row and harvest the roses that were at exactly the right stage of blooming. If the flower head was too tight it wouldn't open, and if it was left on the bush too long, it would open and bloom too soon and would be useless to the florists who purchased them to sell in their shops. It was a delicate balance and Leanne had soon learned when to cut them and when to leave them for another day. Once the harvesting was complete, and the collected flowers were safely stored in the cool room, each variety of rose would be sorted, graded and either discarded if it was imperfect or put into bunches ranging from 30cm posies right up to stunning metre-long stems.

When Leanne wasn't harvesting or bunching, she would do odd jobs such as putting weed mat down around the greenhouses, weeding gardens around the house yard, and throughout the winter months she would prune thousands of dormant roses in the greenhouses that weren't kept heated. It sounded like heaven to me, working amongst a rainbow landscape of perfect flowers, and Leanne often talked about it and told me it was the best job she'd ever had. Sometimes when she was grooming me or putting my rugs on in the evenings she would tell me about her day at work, and my mouth would water imagining how delicious those sweet-smelling roses would taste. Occasionally I liked to eat the big purple flowers off the tall thistles that dotted the paddocks in springtime, but they were so spiky and difficult to chew! Every now and then Leanne would use my lead rope to pull the lilac-coloured flowers off the prickly plant, and she would cut off the nasty sharp spikes that stuck out from each flower with the scissors from her grooming box. It was heaven when I could just enjoy the treat without worrying about getting a splinter in my tongue from it, and if a weed could taste that good just imagine how yummy those soft roses would be!

I must be hungry, I'm getting sidetracked. Back to my story! The people Leanne worked for at the delicious rose farm had told her they were happy for her to bring Frosty and I out to live in one of their paddocks at the front of the property. That way Leanne could simply walk from the greenhouses over to our paddock every day after work to feed and rug us, and she thought that sounded like a great idea! When she told me, I was unsurprised that we were going to be on the move again; I was becoming accustomed to riding the waves of Leanne's somewhat unsettled life and in the wisdom of my old age I was now of the mindset that every time we moved, it brought us one step closer to finding exactly where we were supposed to be in the world. Maybe the rose farm would be the right place for all of us, for Leanne to work among the colourful flowers and for Frosty and I to live so close by that we could watch her comings and goings every day. Besides, if we were living at the rose farm there was actually a chance that I might finally get to sink my teeth into some sweet juicy flowers!

The only bad thing about this latest move was that

it meant we would be leaving our beloved friend Pony behind. When I finally worked up the courage to break the sad news to him, I thought he would be very upset or even angry at being left behind; he was, however, such a kind-hearted old gentleman that he just touched his greying muzzle to mine, snorted softly, nodded at me and gave me an affectionate wink to let me know he was happy for us that we were heading off on our next big adventure. I hoped that we would see each other again one day; he was the most kind, selfless, genuinely good-hearted horse I'd ever met and I knew I would miss him terribly.

Only a few short days later, Frosty and I were officially residents of Bookham. When the truck had arrived to pick us up from Yass, Pony had stayed away. I wanted desperately to see him one more time and tell him I would never forget him, but he didn't like farewells and had decided to leave it at 'see you later' instead of 'goodbye'. I guess somehow it seemed less permanent that way and I understood, but I still desperately looked out across the paddock for him even as I was being led up the ramp onto the truck that would take us away just minutes later. Just like after Moppy went away, I never did get to see Pony again, but I never forgot the sound of his gentle whinny or his warm, sweet familiar scent that had brought me so much comfort throughout our friendship.

The paddock we were put into at Bookham was quite

small, and when we first arrived Frosty became quite distressed. He was a horse that just loved wide open spaces where he could gallop and stretch his neck out into the wind and feel that sense of freedom bursting from within him. As soon as Leanne unclipped his lead rope, he spun around and ran off to explore our new surroundings but was met with disappointment when he reached the fence within seconds. He skidded to a halt quite dramatically, snorted and tossed his head in disgust, then turned and galloped along the fence line as far as it would take him. It wasn't a very big space for both of us but we were here now and we were going to make the best of the opportunity.

Now that Leanne was able to be around more, it was easier for her to go riding every now and then. Sometimes she would saddle Frosty up and ride him around on the big sandy arena that was right across from our paddock. One day, she brought her friend Amanda out to see us. Amanda was very interested in learning to ride and Leanne was going to show her a few things and let her have a go. I'm still not sure why she decided to use Frosty instead of quiet faithful little me; maybe because of that time when she let her cousin ride me and I bolted on her... heehee! Good times.

Anyway, Leanne hopped on Frosty and started walking over to the arena, and as they rode past me at the fence that naughty chestnut gelding looked over at me and gave me a cheeky wink! Oh no, I thought to myself, I wonder what he has got planned for poor unsuspecting Leanne. As it turned out, Leanne was neither poor nor unsuspecting in this situation, as she had fallen victim to Frosty's wild antics too many times over the years to be too relaxed with him! They were trotting around the outside of the arena, and Leanne sat down deeply in the saddle and squeezed her heels to his sides to bring him into a canter. When he was behaving, he would usually sweep smoothly forward into a gorgeous rocking-chair lope that was so slow that Leanne could probably have gotten down from his back and walked along beside him. Today, however, rather than the lope she had been hoping for, Frosty decided to take things up a notch. The second he felt Leanne's heels closing against his sides, he lurched suddenly (and very ungracefully) forward then charged madly into an aggressive canter that was far too fast for arena riding. Leanne pressed the balls of her feet into the stirrups to stabilise herself and pulled back firmly on the reins to slow Frosty down, and he responded by tucking his head down and performing a perfect series of pigroots across the sand.

Amanda had been watching from the side of the arena and her eyes were wide with shock as she watched the rather interesting performance. As Frosty continued his defiant ballet dance, Leanne pulled his head around to force him into a very abrupt circle and roared at him to 'get up, you idiot!'

Frosty seemed very surprised by her sudden change of

demeanour, as if he'd done nothing wrong and it was totally unnecessary for her to be reprimanding him! His wide fluffy ears shot forward and he unexpectedly came to a sudden stop. I snorted with amusement and shook my head affectionately at the silly horse; he was so proud. He was always going to be just a little bit wild, as if he would never allow himself to be completely broken in and as frustrating as he could be at times, it was that spirit that Leanne loved most about him.

Amanda had been waiting for her turn to hop on and try her hand at riding; now after witnessing Leanne's attempts to rein in the mad solid-built quarterhorse, she was very nervous but also couldn't stop laughing at her poor friend. Frosty did calm down after that, and Amanda agreed to have a turn as long as Leanne led her around and promised not to let go. The next day Leanne told me that all the way home from Bookham, Amanda had been laughing and laughing and shouting 'GET UP YOU IDIOT!' at her in the car. The legend of wild Frosty Jack was alive and well and for months afterwards Amanda would bring up the story of the riding lesson-turned rodeo.

Because I was getting quite elderly, when Leanne took me for a ride we wouldn't go too far and she usually didn't even bother putting a saddle on me. Instead, she would just put my pretty bright blue western bridle on me and hop on bareback. She said that she felt bad using my saddle on me because it was so heavy, which it was, and I also appreciated not having the uncomfortable girth pulled tight around me!

We would usually just wander through one of the various paddocks on the property, and it was very pretty scenery. One afternoon we had been exploring one of the large lower paddocks, and Leanne spotted a sheep trail that stretched out up the hill to a gate that stood right outside the greenhouses where the roses grew. It reminded her of the good old 'bolting hill' from our days at Macarthur, and I was absolutely thrilled when she turned me towards it and urged me forward into a canter. I sailed joyfully up the hill, cantering slowly at first but then gaining speed until I broke into a gallop. My legs stretched out beneath me and we sailed along, Leanne leaning forward with the reins resting in her hands about halfway up my neck as she laughed in the wind. When we reached the top of the hill Leanne pulled me up just before the gate, and there on the other side of the fence was her boss, Don, gawking at us in surprise. He'd been crouching down in the long grass trying to repair a broken pipe and had been suddenly interrupted by the unexpected thunder of approaching hooves! He looked quite comical, the way he popped up out of nowhere like a meerkat, his eyes wide with surprise, dirt smeared across his face and a stray piece of dead grass sticking out of his hair, and Leanne couldn't help but laugh. She gave him a friendly wave, patted me on the neck to thank me for the gallop, and we turned and headed back down the hill towards my paddock.

That was such a fun afternoon and even though the uphill run had left me feeling very worn out, I was so glad we did it. I lived for those moments of freedom and excitement with her; they were like a little glimpse of the young Leanne, and certainly much younger me, coming back to life and all through the night when I fell asleep that night I dreamt of gliding through green paddocks and sailing over jumps with Leanne laughing on my back. Those were the days.

One thing I remember about Bookham was that there were a lot of sheep, and during lambing season the paddocks were dotted with little playful white lambs leaping and bucking and bleating for their mothers. They sure were cute little suckers and I loved to stand at the fence and watch them playing in the sunshine. One day when Leanne came to feed Frosty and I, she noticed a sheep lying in one of the yards near our paddock. She wandered over to see what had happened, and there on the ground lay a pretty merino ewe. She had blood coming from her back end and she was very weak and cold. It was starting to rain and the poor sheep was shivering uncontrollably. It looked as if she had run into some trouble having a lamb and she probably wouldn't survive; neither of her bosses were home to help but Leanne felt so sorry for the poor thing that she jogged over to the shed where she kept her horse gear and grabbed one of my spare waterproof rugs. She carried it back across to the ewe, and gently laid it over her to protect her from the cold weather and spots of rain that were starting to fall. She gave the frightened ewe a quick pat and wished her well, then left her alone so as not to distress her any further. She finished making our feeds and went home, and forgot about the dying sheep until a few days later. She was working away putting bunches of roses together in the packing shed when Don suddenly said to her 'Leanne, I've been meaning to ask you. Did you put a rug over that sheep that was in the yards the other day?'. At first Leanne thought she was going to be in trouble; some graziers don't like to 'interfere' with their sheep, particularly when it comes to lambing, so she was worried that she had done the wrong thing. To her relief, rather than tell her off Don thanked her. He said they'd had to pull her lamb because it had become stuck when it was being born, and he'd expected the ewe to be dead by the time he got home that day. Instead, when he'd returned she was warm and dry under the rug Leanne had put over her and was still alive; she ended up getting to her feet later that evening and had survived! I was very glad to hear that it had ended well, although I'm not sure what became of the lamb they'd had to pull from her.

Chapter 22 – 10 happy years and counting

Early one afternoon in mid-September of 2008, I was standing in my paddock enjoying the soft springtime sunshine on my back when I saw Leanne's ute pull up at the gate. I put my ears forward and walked over to her eagerly, as I was feeling quite hungry and I assumed she was here to feed me. She got out of the shiny little blue ute with a big smile on her face, opened the gate and gave me a huge cuddle. 'Happy 10-year anniversary baby girl!' she cried excitedly as she hugged me, with her arms wrapped around my shoulders and her cheek resting against my neck. She let go and gave me a big kiss on the nose, and she told me that today it was exactly 10 years since the day she had gotten me. My head was spinning thinking how quickly those 10 whole years had gone by, and how many fantastic and very precious memories we had made together in that time. I was so touched that she had actually remembered our 'anniversary' that a little buzz of happiness tingled down my spine. I felt all warm and fuzzy; how special this seemingly ordinary day had suddenly become! Little did I know, it was about to get even better. First, Leanne went over to the passenger side of her ute, opened the door and came back with my halter and 2 party hats. She put the halter on me and led me out of the paddock onto the grass near where she'd parked, and although I wasn't all that impressed about it, I stood patiently while she carefully placed one of the cardboard party hats on my head. It was white with pictures of coloured balloons all over it, and there it was, stuck on my head right between my ears. I must have looked ridiculous but I didn't care, this was a very special occasion! Leanne stood back to admire my party hat, laughed delightedly, and then placed the other hat on her own head. Then she went back to the ute to get something else, and I stood there hoping it wasn't going to be a giant pair of sunglasses or a feather boa or something silly like that; you wouldn't know what sort of crazy ideas this girl might get in her head sometimes!

I was standing there waiting to see what she was going to do to me next, when I heard the sound of giggling coming from the paddock. Oh no, Frosty had spotted me wearing the ridiculous hat and he was laughing at me! I looked over at him and he nodded his big fat head up and down and then stuck his top lip right up in the air, his enormous pink gums showing as he jeered at me with amusement. I swished my tail at him and tossed my head to tell him to go away, and then quickly turned my attention back to Leanne because a delicious, familiar smell had suddenly come floating into my nostrils. To my absolute delight, I saw that she was carrying my most favourite special treat ever in the whole world – one of her homemade puddings! I was so excited that I whinnied and immediately stretched out my neck to reach it so I could take a bite. I was disappointed at first, because she quickly moved it away from me and said 'hang on a minute, we need to get a photo!'. Leanne had organised for her friend Jean, who also worked at the rose farm, to meet us there and take some photos for her, and even though I was a bit embarrassed to be seen wearing a party hat, it was a very special moment in my life so I didn't mind posing for some pictures. I only had to wait for a minute or so before I was finally allowed to sink my teeth into the delicious pudding, and it was pure heaven. It was a big mound made of soggy bread that she had mixed together with apple sauce, sugar cubes, carrot sticks and chunks of crunchy juicy apple, and each bite tasted even yummier than the last. I didn't even care that I was making a guts of myself, I pigged down every last bit of it! While this was all happening, Don's wife Sarah had been walking past in her garden and was surprised to see Leanne and I standing there wearing our matching party hats. She laughed when she spotted us, and then called out to Leanne 'I've got a bottle of champagne in the fridge if you want it for your party over there!'. Leanne and Jean laughed, and I was a tiny bit disappointed that they didn't accept the offer and enjoy a glass of bubbly with our celebrations. I've never had champagne, I would have liked to try some! Leanne had the photos of our anniversary party printed out and she told me she had stuck one on her fridge where she could look at it every day, and it always made her smile. I knew how she felt, because every time I thought about that day it made me smile too.

Because we were in a fairly small paddock at Bookham, it didn't take long for us to eat down all of the grass that was in there. It hadn't been raining very much for the previous few months, so even when we first moved in there hadn't been a great deal of feed for us to graze on anyway. To my delight, Leanne started bringing big tubs full of rose scraps from the packing shed for us to eat! When they put together the bunches of roses during sorting and packing, they would run the bottom half of the stems through a machine that removed all of the thorns and leaves. Those leaves would be collected in big white oval-shaped tubs at the end of every day and instead of dumping them out behind the packing shed, Leanne put them in the back of her ute and drove them up to our paddock. Frosty and I would stand at the fence watching and waiting for her to finish work, and we would toss our heads and prance excitedly when we finally saw her driving up the dusty gravel road from the greenhouses.

The leaves were delicious; sweet, easy to chew, and they were a perfect (and cost-effective) way to fill our hungry bellies. Sometimes there were even silky soft sweet roses hidden in the tubs, which were the best treat of all. When I would spot one amongst the leaves, I always tried to grab it before that piggy Frosty saw it – age before beauty, after all! Each rose I ever got to eat was exactly as delicious and satisfying as I'd imagined they would be back when Leanne used to tell me about them. I loved the pale orange Valencia variety the best; they had the most incredible perfume and when I bit into the flower head the intense yet somehow delicate flavour washed over my tastebuds and filled my whole mouth with a sweetness that was sent straight from heaven! There weren't usually many though, because when roses were rejected during sorting Leanne or Jean would often take them home and put them in a vase in their house. Can you imagine that? Fancy wasting such a rare tasty treat by sticking it in a glass of water in your house and never even eating it! Humans do such odd things at times.

On weekends when Leanne didn't work at the rose farm, she would drive from home to feed Frosty and I each afternoon and she would usually bring her dog. It was a funny-looking little cattle dog she had named Dawg, and it had a blue-heeler coloured body with red-heeler coloured legs. Dawg's head was also red and it looked too small for her body, as if it had been stuck on haphazardly when someone was carelessly building a dog from leftover parts. She had never been around horses until Leanne got her, and at first she didn't seem to be worried by us at all. Sometimes when I would be eating my dinner, Dawg would wander over and sit down in the shade underneath me with her side resting against my back leg. She seemed like a happy friendly little dog and I quite liked her-until the day she attacked me, that is!

Just like every other weekend, Leanne had driven out to see us and had made our dinner feeds, and while she waited for us to finish eating she was letting Dawg have a wander around the paddock. Dawg was sniffing around my bucket, eating up some of the pellets I had dropped, and then she wandered over to stand in the shade beneath me as she often liked to do. My bucket had slid forwards along the ground while I was eating, so I took a step forward to be able to reach it easier. As I moved, I must have startled the dog and I was shocked and frightened when completely out of the blue, she snarled and latched onto my back leg. She bit down very hard, growling angrily as she attacked me, and I squealed with fright, swung my leg away from her and ran off into the paddock. My heart was pounding and I could feel my poor leg stinging where her teeth had cut into me. Leanne had seen what happened and she was just as surprised by Dawg's sudden aggression as I was; she was also very angry. She shouted furiously at the dog to 'come here!' and marched towards her, but Dawg was well aware of the fact that she was in serious trouble and she went slinking off into the paddock with her tail between her legs, her head down and her ears flat on her head. Leanne continued to demand that the dog come to her, and eventually the naughty frightened dog laid down on her belly and allowed Leanne to grab her by the collar and take her back to the ute. Leanne made her jump up onto the tray and clipped the short chain to her collar angrily, and then she took a minute to tell Dawg what a bad dog she was. Then she turned her attention back to me; I was still standing over in the spot where I had run to after I was bitten, with my ears pinned back and my lower lip trembling as I stomped my injured leg on the ground unhappily. Leanne walked over and stroked my face gently, offering me a calming 'shhhh' as she leaned down to see what the dog had done. There on my fetlock were 2 cuts; puncture wounds from the stupid mutt's big canine teeth, and one of the wounds was bleeding quite a lot. Leanne's facial expression had now changed from concern into fury, and she looked over at the dog sitting on the ute and glared fiercely at her; if looks could kill, that dog would have been a goner for sure. Boy was she cranky! She gave me a quick pat and told me to finish the rest of my dinner, then she walked quickly up to the shed where she kept all of our gear. When she returned a couple of minutes later she was carrying some saline and a can of antiseptic spray. She pulled the top off the plastic bottle of saline solution and squirted it all over my bite wounds to clean them, and then she carefully sprayed the antiseptic on them to kill any germs and hopefully stop the cuts from getting infected. That antiseptic spray sure did sting, and as soon as I felt it hit my wounds I lifted my leg up under my belly and tried to keep it away from her. I was so annoyed at that mean, nasty dog; I thought we were friends, how could she do this to me?

Leanne didn't bring Dawg to see us for a while after that. She was uncertain about exactly why the dog had bitten me, but the more she thought about it the more it seemed like Dawg has just gotten a fright when I stepped forward and reacted accordingly, so she decided to give her another chance and hope it was a one-off. She didn't seem like an aggressive type of dog. Unfortunately, that mean little Dawg ended up blowing her second chance. She had only been al-lowed to come with Leanne to feed us again a couple of times when her mean streak reared its ugly head again, but this time it wasn't me that was attacked. It was Frosty!

He was happily stuffing his face with his dinner, chewing contentedly and minding his own business, when Dawg came wandering up and started sniffing around on the ground near his bucket. Now Frosty was the friendliest horse you'd ever meet, he wanted to be buddies with everyone and would rarely ever pin his ears back or be even the slightest bit rude to another animal. When he noticed that the dog was right beside him, he was curious and stretched out his friendly big boof head to sniff at her and say hello. Within a split second of poor old Frosty attempting to greet her, that wicked dog whirled around and then CHOMP! She lurched forward and latched onto him, right on the end of his muzzle.

Frosty was absolutely petrified and he squealed with fright and went scrambling backwards madly, almost falling over his own feet as he tried to get away from the nasty mutt. His kind brown eyes that were usually soft and gentle were now rolling wildly back in his head and he snorted in terror and went galloping off, as far away as he could get from the vicious Dawg. I thought Leanne had been mad when the dog had bitten me, but when it happened for the second time she absolutely snapped. She was so furiously angry that I thought steam might have started coming out of her ears at any second. I could feel the rage beaming out of her as she roared at the now-cowering dog to get back on the ute. The dog once again knew she was in big trouble, and she repeated her slinking flat-eared routine as she made her way to the ute and jumped up. As Leanne stormed over to her, Dawg tried her hardest to make friends again by sitting up straight, smiling and panting and madly thumping the tip of her tail on the ute, wagging it as if appearing to be a good happy dog might save her from being reprimanded. Well, she was out of luck because at that moment Leanne had absolutely no interest in being friendly with her. She roared and ranted as she gruffly clipped the chain onto Dawg's collar, and the cowardly hound just laid down on her belly and wouldn't even look Leanne in the eye. After Leanne had finished telling her off, she came back over to inspect poor old Frosty Jack's nose. She was so upset when she saw that the beautiful spirited gelding had 4 puncture wounds as a result of the attack; a hole from each of the dog's canine teeth, 2 in his top lip and 2 in his bottom lip. She did her best to clean them and treat them but Frosty was a very flighty horse by nature and he was still too shaken up to cooperate and let her help him. He ended up healing just fine, as did my leg, but Leanne never brought the unpredictable Dawg with her to see us ever again. She had done her dash, and over time Leanne discovered that while she was a lovely dog to people and was great with kids, she was very prone to attacking when it came to animals, especially other dogs, and she had to be kept away to avoid any more unpleasant incidents.

Towards the end of the year, when Christmas was rapidly approaching and the summer weather was starting to heat things up, Leanne and Jean were given some sad news. Things were getting tough in the florist industry and Don and Sarah could no longer afford to keep employing them. The girls would finish up permanently when trading stopped for the Christmas break; this also meant that Leanne now had to find a new place for us to live, again. Leanne was very sad to be losing her job working amongst the stunning rainbow of roses, but times were hard for everyone so all she could do was stay positive and keep looking ahead to brighter days. Leanne's boyfriend Greg had recently purchased a house in the small village of Binalong, only about 15-minutes drive from Bookham, which they were both now living in so Leanne started looking for a paddock for us closer to her new home. It didn't take too long before she was offered a property for Frosty and I to live on, only a couple of minutes from her house, and it wouldn't even cost her anything for agistment! The owners of the 70-acre property lived there, but they didn't have any stock and wanted to keep the long grass down. They were more than happy to have a couple of horses there to graze the paddocks, so it was arranged for Frosty and I to move in. I knew I would miss getting to eat roses sometimes, but I was looking forward to having a bit more space and being closer to Leanne again!

Don and Sarah kindly offered to use their float to transport us over to Binalong; Don assured Leanne that he would drive very slowly and carefully so that I hopefully wouldn't fall again, and a couple of weeks before Christmas we once again strapped on our big padded boots and tail bandages and loaded up. The drive didn't take long, and I'm happy to say that we both travelled just fine and arrived in one piece. When we got to our new home, a lovely shady property on a road called Cattle Street, I backed slowly and awkwardly down the ramp off the float and looked around nervously; I wondered what this place would hold for us. As I was led through the gate into our new paddock, a strange, comforting yet somehow still unsettling feeling washed over me; there was something different about this place. I raised my head and looked around, breathing in the smell of pine needles and cool fresh bushland air, and I suddenly knew deep down in my heart that I would never leave this place. This was going to be where I would stay.

Chapter 23 - Binalong

It didn't take long for us to settle in amongst the rolling hills of Cattle Street. The 70-acre property was divided into 3 large paddocks which were shoulder-deep with feed, and it was only Frosty and I living there to enjoy it all! We spent the first few days gorging ourselves silly, eating and eating until I thought we might both turn into a patch of grass, we ate so much. We were so full that we weren't even interested in eating the delicious feeds Leanne brought us, and after a while we were so fat and round that we didn't need feeding and she would only bring us a few carrots and apples for a treat when she checked on us every afternoon!

Sometimes Leanne would saddle me up and ride me down the road to her house, where she would close her front gate and leave me to graze in the front yard for a few hours before she would take me back again. I loved our peaceful little rides, but the problem with taking me out was that Frosty would get very, very upset. He must have been worried that I wouldn't come back, and for the whole time that I was gone he would trot back and forth along the fence line, neighing loudly and tossing his head in distress. He hated being left on his own and we could hear him calling out all the way from Leanne's front yard. When we were on our way back, he would hear the sound of my hooves clip-clopping up the road and he would whinny and snort and behave as if we had been gone for 3 years rather than 3 hours. As proud and wild as Frosty was, he was still a big softie at heart and he really was a sook when he was left alone.

One fine day when the sun was shining and the sky was a clear crisp blue, Leanne decided she would ride Frosty into town for a look around. It was a little bit too far to take me at my age, as much as I would have loved to go. To get to the small but picturesque main street of the little village, Leanne would have to cross a very busy main road that was always rushing with huge trucks, noisy motorbikes and a never-ending stream of cars. She was quite worried about how Frosty would handle it and whether or not he would behave himself, but when it came time to cross the dreaded road he was actually very good. He was tense, and very nervous, but he wasn't skittish; he walked quietly across the highway and they continued on along the grass towards the Binalong village centre.

One thing he didn't like at all was the tall green wheelie bins that stood silently at the top of some of the driveways; Moppy had hated them too back when we lived at Macarthur! As Frosty passed each bin, he would snort with fear and keep one ear firmly locked on the direction of the bin, and as he was almost past it he would quickly dart forwards as if he thought a gremlin was going to jump out and grab him. Luckily there wasn't too many horrifiyingly dangerous wheelie bins out that day so Frosty didn't end up being eaten by one. When they got to the main street, it was very quiet and Frosty's hooves sounded surprisingly loud as they wandered up the road of the sleepy town. As they passed the garage, Frosty shied at the unfamiliar smell of petrol and grease, and he snorted loudly as he attempted to blow the strange odour out of his nose.

On their left was a humble general store with fading newspaper and ice cream signs hanging in the windows, and on the front door were stickers advertising products that had stopped being manufactured years earlier. It was the kind of welcoming, yesteryear-type store where kids would go after school to buy bags of colourful mixed lollies, and the locals had been faithfully calling in there to buy their bread and milk every morning for decades. Frosty continued on, past a tiny rural store where Leanne sometimes bought our chaff and pellets, and on their right was a neat little building that housed the butchery; displayed proudly on the large sign above the doorway there was a painting of a Brahman bull, which was also the mascot of the local football team, the Binalong Brahmans. Frosty kept clip-clopping nervously towards the post office that stood opposite the tall red-brick façade of the local watering hole, Hotel Binalong, at the end of the street. On the corner diagonally across from the post office was a beautiful heritage-type building which proclaimed 'General Storekeeper' across the front in large old-fashioned lettering. Looming over either side of the shop's shady front entrance were 2 enormous Bunya pine trees, which stood silently at attention with their tips so high up above the rooftop that they seemed to almost be touching the clouds. The shop had long been a general store previously, but these days inside the stunning old building was a busy café. Frosty's nostrils had filled with the smell of espresso coffee and takeaway food, which he seemed to enjoy far more than the strange smells of the garage, and he peered in the direction of the café curiously. There were people sitting outside on a sunny deck enjoying their coffee, and they gave Leanne a friendly wave as they commented to each other about the handsome solid-built chestnut horse who was staring at them with such fascination.

They wandered on up the street and when they got to the front of the post office Leanne dismounted, thinking she would check her mail while she was here. The mail didn't get delivered to houses in Binalong, it all went straight to the post office and the residents would go in to collect it when they were in town. What Leanne hadn't really considered with her plan though, was what she was going to do with Frosty when she went inside to get the mail! She stood there for a minute, looking at Frosty, then looking at the door to the post office which was up a small flight of concrete stairs a few metres away, and while she was trying to decide if she was game to tie him up to the handrail of the steps, Frosty kept his gaze firmly on the interesting-smelling café. His stomach grumbled and he tossed his head and tried to start walking back over towards the source of the delicious food smells, but Leanne told him to stand, so he drooped his fluffy ears and stood there sulking instead. Leanne decided it probably wasn't a good idea to tie him up just in case he got a fright and pulled back; he might snap his reins and go bolting off through the streets, and that would be a disaster. She ended up calling out from the side door of the post office and the friendly lady inside brought out her mail, a few small envelopes that she stuffed into her pocket. Frosty told me that she said it was 'probably just bills' so he wasn't sure why she took it; we didn't even know who 'Bill' was!

When Leanne and Frosty returned from their big adventure into town, I was so pleased to see them! I hadn't been neighing and pacing and getting upset like Frosty did whenever I went out, but I'd certainly felt lonely and agitated while he was gone. When I saw them coming back through the gate I whinnied excitedly and trotted over to them, sniffing at Frosty and bursting to hear all about what he'd seen. After Leanne had put our rugs on for the night and given us each a very small feed (we were fatties remember), she said goodbye to us and told us she'd see us tomorrow, and she headed home for the night. As soon as she was gone I started hassling Frosty to tell me all about the ride; where did they go, what did he see, what was it like? It had been years since I'd been into a town area like that and I wondered if it was similar to the shops I'd seen when Leanne and I had our hot-chip picnic at Fadden Pines way back in our younger days. As Frosty told me all the details of the terrifying wheelie bins, the weird stinky garage, and the mouth-watering smells of the café, I could picture it all in my mind so clearly and I hoped I would get to see it all for myself one day. I nodded off to sleep that night dreaming about sipping on a bucket of cappuccino in the sun, outside the busy little café with the sky-scraping Bunya pines quietly standing guard beside it.

Leanne had never been able to find out for sure exactly how old I was; my previous owner Veronica had told her that I was about 18 years old at the time when Leanne first bought me from her, but then a dentist who filed my teeth had said he thought I was slightly older than that. I hadn't kept count, but the general consensus was that I was somewhere in my early 30's. That's getting pretty old for a horse, and I was really starting to feel it. All through the harsh frost-bitten winter of 2009 I struggled to keep warm and found it very difficult to get back up on my feet if I had been lying down. My joints ached, I was always stiff and sore and some days I spent more time asleep than awake. Leanne made sure I had nice comfy rugs on that would keep me as dry and toasty warm as possible, but it seemed like the cold that year seeped right into my very bones. Thank goodness there was plenty of feed in our paddock to sustain us through those freezing dreary months; the roughage we grazed on throughout the day kept us warm from the inside as it heated up in our bellies and it definitely helped me get through the long cold nights.

After what seemed like an eternity, finally winter broke and we started to feel warmth sneaking back into the midday sunshine. Patches of clover were popping up amongst the grass and high up in their nests we could hear baby birds squawking frantically at their parents to put food into their empty bellies. With the faint familiar scent of golden wattle drifting on the breeze, I took a deep breath and sighed with relief; spring was here! I had made it through one more winter.

One morning, Leanne turned up to see me and I could tell straight away that something was different about her. I stood watching her approach with my one good eye, and tried to work out what had changed. Had she had a haircut? No, it looked the same. Was she wearing different clothes? Again, no, it was her usual type of outfit. She came up and greeted me and as she put my halter on, I felt her tummy bumping against me. That was weird, I thought. Why is her belly sticking out like that? She must have eaten a very big breakfast! We wandered up to the gate together, Frosty faithfully trailing along behind us, and Leanne told me that she had some big news to tell us. I sniffed at her, wondering what could possibly be going on, and I was very surprised when she turned to face me and said 'I'm going to have a baby!'.

A baby? Leanne was going to have a baby? Well how on earth that happened I did not know, but I was very shocked and unsure of how to feel about it! Apparently so was Leanne, because we had a very long conversation about it and she said that it had come as a huge surprise to her and she was feeling very frightened and overwhelmed. She talked and talked while she absent-mindedly brushed my silver coat and pulled sticks out of my tail, and I listened and listened while I absent-mindedly chewed on my lucerne chaff, not really even tasting it I was so distracted. At first I felt upset, maybe even a little bit jealous, concerned at how much things might change for us if she was busy with a new baby all the time. I liked our casual, relaxed lifestyle and I didn't want anything to change! But the more I thought about it, the more I realised that this was exactly how I had reacted when I found out about Leanne getting Moppy, and then again when I found out she was getting Frosty, and both times it had turned out great! Moppy and Frosty had certainly brought big changes to our lives, but they had been happy changes and I wouldn't have swapped them for anything. I was sure that although it might take a bit of getting used to, this tiny little person growing inside Leanne's rounding belly would be a blessing to all of us and by the end of the day I'd decided I couldn't wait to meet him or her.

Leanne's belly continued to get bigger as the months rolled by, and before we knew it spring had been and gone and summer was moving in. These days the heat knocked me around even more than the cold and I knew it was going to be tough on my poor worn-out old body. One stuffy afternoon, Leanne arrived and stood at the top of the property calling out to us. Frosty had heard her, and he started walking eagerly towards her, but then he stopped and looked behind him, wondering if I was going to come with him. I was lying down in a soft patch of dusty dirt, flat out on my side with my head resting on the ground, in a very deep sleep. My hearing was very poor, almost non-existent by that stage, and I hadn't even heard Leanne's calls. Frosty had snorted at me and pawed at the ground with his front foot impatiently, but he was unable to wake me up. Leanne continued to call out to us, and from where she had been standing she started walking down into the paddock to see if she could spot us. When she got about halfway down the paddock, she caught sight of us and she suddenly froze. Frosty was standing there, pawing at the dirt and looking quite distressed, and she could see the shape of me lying on the ground, unmoving. Her heart leapt into her throat and she yelled out to me, but I didn't hear her and I didn't move or react. Frosty tossed his head unhappily, confused and unsure of what he should do. Leanne stood there watching me for a moment, terrified of what she was about to find, and then she started running towards me. She was holding onto her big round belly as she jogged as fast as her awkward pregnant body would allow, and as she made her way through the spiky dry summer grass she screamed out to me desperately. I laid there, still not moving. No response at all. By now Leanne was crying, big fat terrified tears streaming down her cheeks, as she raced through the paddock. Frosty stared at her with wide frightened eyes as he watched her getting closer, and he sniffed at me and trotted in a circle around me. Leanne was crying her eyes out and when she was about 5 metres away from where I was lying, she screamed out to me again... and this time the sound of her voice cut into my dream and startled me awake.

I suddenly sat up, unsure of what was happening, and there in front of me was poor Leanne sobbing uncontrollably. As soon as she saw me move and realised I was alive, she was so relieved that she sobbed even more. I had given her the fright of her life; she'd thought I was gone. Still feeling dazed, I slowly dragged myself to my feet and shook the dust from my coat, and Leanne stepped forward and gave me the world's biggest cuddle. She had been so scared! We all walked very slowly together up the hill to our waiting feed buckets, and while I ate, Leanne brushed me and told me how terrifying it had been not knowing if I was alright or not. I hadn't realised until she told me that day that it was something she often thought about and worried over; I was getting so old, and she was frightened that she would come out one day and find that I had slipped away during the night. I sometimes worried about how much more time I had left, but it hadn't occurred to me that she worried about it too.

At the height of summer, we ran into a big problem. There were 2 large dams on the property that were our only source of water, and they had both dried up. All that was left of them was a tiny miserable puddle surrounded by dangerous sticky mud. For several weeks, Leanne had no choice but to cart water to us from her house. She had gotten hold of half a dozen large buckets with lids, and she would sit them all on the back of her ute, fill them up from her hose, then seal on the lids and drive them up to us on Cattle Street. Then she would have to try to get the heavy buckets off the ute and tip them into an old bathtub just inside the paddock gate. On really hot days she would have to do 2 runs of water, morning and afternoon, because we would drink so much, and it also evaporated quickly in the sun. Lifting the buckets was very difficult for her in her heavily pregnant state, and after a while she decided that in an attempt to cut down on how much water she had to cart, she would take me down to live in her large front yard until it rained and the dams refilled. That way she would only have to take water up once a day because it would last longer with only one horse drinking it. She led me down to her house late one evening when the soaring temperatures were starting to drop, and all the way there I could hear Frosty whinnying frantically to me from up on the hill. She had been worried about separating us, but she was hoping that after a day or 2 things would settle down and it wouldn't cause too much of a problem. Unfortunately for her, it didn't settle down and it caused a very big problem!

When I first got to her yard, I had a drink from a big blue tub she had filled up for me, and then I wandered about looking for grass to eat. The summertime heat had baked the front lawn into a miserable patch of dry, brittle dead weeds, but along the edge of the creek Leanne lived on there was a little bit of grass growing. It didn't take me very long to munch my way through the best bits, and then I looked up and noticed that the sun was going down and it was almost dark. This was not right! I snorted fiercely and trotted up to the front fence, then I threw my head up and neighed as loudly as I could. Off in the distance, I heard the very faint reply of Frosty's whinny and I started to become very distressed. I neighed back to him, over and over again, and I started to pace up and down with frustration.

Along the front fence, Leanne had lovingly planted about a dozen rose bushes of all different colours a few months earlier. She had been given them when they were replacing some of the varieties at the rose farm and she had thought they would look pretty growing across the front of the yard. Well, at the time I couldn't care less about those stupid roses and in my panic to get back to Frosty I stomped right over them all. With big agitated strides I paced, up and down, up and down along the fence, and under my hooves the rose bushes were trampled mercilessly into the dirt. All night I paced and whinnied, and snorted and kicked, and by the time Leanne came out the next morning her lovely row of roses was completely destroyed. She had barely gotten any sleep overnight, partly because she was so big and uncomfortable being just weeks away from her baby's due date, but mainly because of the racket I had caused with my incessant neighing. She had stomped grumpily down the front stairs, rubbing at her tired eyes and yawning, and when she saw what I had done she froze in her tracks. It had taken hours to dig the holes for all those roses, and to plant them and fertilise them and keep them watered through the hot summer days, and in a single night I had ruined them. I don't even know what I was so agitated about, it wasn't like me to be that concerned about being separated from other horses. Maybe I was getting insecure in my old age, or maybe I was upset because I knew Frosty would be stressing too. Either way, Leanne's rose garden, her pretty display of her favourite flowers, was smashed into a mess of broken sticks in the dirt. By the end of that day, Leanne had taken me back up to my paddock on Cattle Street and she had arranged for Greg to come up and help her do the water buckets every afternoon. Frosty and I were back together again and that was the way we liked it!

Early in March of 2010, we didn't see Leanne for a few

days. This was out of character for her; she would usually always come up and check on us, even if we didn't need feeding. Every afternoon I would stand patiently at the gate, peering down the road waiting to see her driving up the hill, and for those few days I was left disappointed when she never arrived. Then early one afternoon I caught a glimpse of someone walking towards me through the long grass, and to my surprise and delight, I saw that she was here... and she was carrying a tiny new baby! My heart skipped a beat and I swished my tail nervously as I walked quickly towards them. The big day I had waited months for was finally here; I was actually going to meet Leanne's baby! As I got closer, I saw that the tiny brand new little person was fast asleep, blissfully unaware of anything going on in the world around them. I reached out to sniff gently at Leanne and the little bundle in her arms, and she said 'he's finally here!'

He? It was a boy! I couldn't wait for him to get a bit bigger so we could be buddies! Leanne carefully placed the sleeping baby back in his car seat and then got our buckets of feed off the back of the ute. She spent a few minutes watching Frosty and I eat and giving us both an affectionate scratch on the neck, and then she said she was very tired and she'd better go home. As I watched her driving away, I started to imagine a little cowboy in jeans and boots learning to ride, sitting high up on my back where he could see the whole world at his feet. I could picture him helping Leanne carry our buckets, and standing at my side reaching up as high as he could to help with brushing me. Leanne had certainly looked very tired, but she had also looked incredibly impossibly happy, and a feeling of contentment washed over me as I dozed off to sleep under the pine trees that evening. I think I already loved that little boy.

Every afternoon from then on, when Leanne would come to see us, she would bring my sleepy little cowboy buddy with her. She told me he didn't really like to be put down or be away from her, and she spent most of her time cuddling him or feeding him. He smelled lovely; I'd never sniffed a baby before but somehow the scent of him seemed familiar, as if it reminded me of something I'd forgotten about years ago. The more I got to see him, the more I adored him and I was bursting with excitement to see him get bigger and start walking, and then start riding! He had no hair, just a fine layer of peach-fuzz fluff lightly covering his round head, and he had huge blue eyes that blinked at me with surprise the first time I greeted him when he was actually awake. I was an old horse made young again by love; love for my best friend of so many years, and love for this tiny little soul that she had brought into our lives. Life had never been better.

Chapter 24 -

I'm afraid I'm not feeling very well today. I'm frightened... I think something may be very wrong with me. It's as if my legs won't do what I want them to, it's hard to breathe and my head feels like it's filled with a heavy fog. I laid down overnight to rest, hoping I would feel better this morning, but now I can't find the strength to stand up again... I'm not sure what's going to happen. Something is very wrong... I'm sorry, I had better go and try to rest again. I'll continue my story for you another day friends. Goodbye.

Dear reader,

My name is Leanne, and I'm sorry to tell you that on Tuesday the 18th of May 2010, I had to say goodbye to my best friend of 12 years; Consuela.

I arrived at the paddock on Cattle Street at about 10:30 in the morning, planning to take rugs off; it was a clear sunny day and I thought the horses would enjoy the sunshine on their coats. When I got there, it took me quite a while to find them. I couldn't see Consuela, but I had spotted Frosty standing in the far bottom corner of the property. I called out to him but he just stared at me and wouldn't move, so I got in my car and drove down the paddock towards him. When I got a bit closer I realised that Consuela was lying on the ground at Frosty's feet, and I instantly knew that something was wrong.

There were marks in the dirt where she had dragged herself all the way down the hill overnight, in her attempts to get back on her feet. She had given up once she found herself stuck against the boundary fence, and she had been laying there waiting for help ever since. She was alive, but she was obviously very unwell. I tried to help her stand up, and she really wanted to, she tried so hard, but she was too weak and she had been down for too long. I had no mobile phone service in that area at the time, so I was devastated to have to leave her there in distress and drive home to ring for help. I called a vet who lives just out of Binalong and arranged for her to come straight out, and then I called a local woman who lived around the corner. I didn't really even know her that well back then; I hardly knew anyone in Binalong in those days. This woman I rang was always very friendly and she had horses and would understand my situation, so I called to ask if she would come up and help look after my baby son while the vet tended to Consuela. I was so grateful when she instantly said of course she would come and help. I hung up and then I rushed back to be at my faithful little mare's side.

The vet came, and decided to give Consuela a big dose of painkillers to see if that would help her get to her feet. If she was down because of an injury, the medication might ease her pain enough that she could stand and we could treat her. We tried and tried, and so did Consuela; she fought fiercely to get up and used every last scrap of energy she could find, but it was all in vain. She was completely unable to stand anymore, and there was nothing else we could do for her. The decision I had been dreading was made; I had to put her down.

I don't think the reality of what was happening actually hit me until the vet started injecting the euthanasia drug into her. I was stroking her face and trying to keep her calm, despite the fact that I could barely even see her through my tears and I was a complete mess, and I can vividly remember looking down at the menacing dark green solution in the syringe and starting to sob uncontrollably. Behind us, over in the paddock, stood the lovely local woman I'd called for help; she was rocking my tiny son gently in her arms, and he was crying. He was just 11 weeks old on the day that Consuela died, and the dreams that I'd had for both of them were shattered before they'd even begun.

Frosty refused to leave Consuela's side throughout the entire ordeal, and for 3 weeks afterwards he was a mess, galloping around the paddocks in distress calling out for his lost friend. Consuela was buried there in that secluded corner of the Cattle Street property where she had spent her final moments. It's a peaceful, quiet place surrounded by gnarled old gum trees and there is the constant sound of kookaburras laughing and rosellas squabbling amongst the treetops above her. I just hope she's not lonely there. I will never know exactly what went wrong for Consuela in the end; all I know is that she was very old, she was incredibly loved, and she had lived a most extraordinary life.

Consuela really was the horse of my dreams; the culmination of all the years of my childhood spent begging my parents to buy me a horse of my very own. She was the horse every little girl dreams of owning. The horse that you could climb onto the back of and go running off into the wind, and truly feel as if your soul had been set free. She was the horse that sets a fire in your heart that never goes out, and no matter how hard things got, she was always there waiting for me. She was a constant light burning brightly and warmly through the ebbs and flows of my life as I grew into an adult, and I cannot imagine what things would have been like without her throughout those years.

I always dreamed of horses as a child, and thanks to that incredible little mare I know that I will still, always, dream of horses.

There are countless days and moments of my time with her that have been forgotten, pushed from my memory by the constraints of time and the chaos of life, but there are so many beautiful moments that I've remembered and it has been a soul-shaking journey reliving so many of them for you throughout the creation of this book. Thanks for saddling up with us, and I hope you've enjoyed the ride as much as I did. It's been an honour to share with you the story of Consuela, the best horse I will ever know.

Leanne.